The Last Mutineers

Prequel

By: Patrick M. Bedont Jr.

PRINTED IN THE UNITED STATES OF AMERICA

FIRST PRINTING: 2017

ISBN-13: 978-0-9990350-2-3

ISBN-10: 0-9990350-2-9

TEPBIAN KORD PUBLISHING
9030 NARLEK BASE ROAD
TORN HUND NOTHING, PA 15642

THELASTMUTINEERS.COM
MINDS.COM/MISANTHROMEME
LINKTR.EE/TEPBIANKORD

❴«•2•»❵

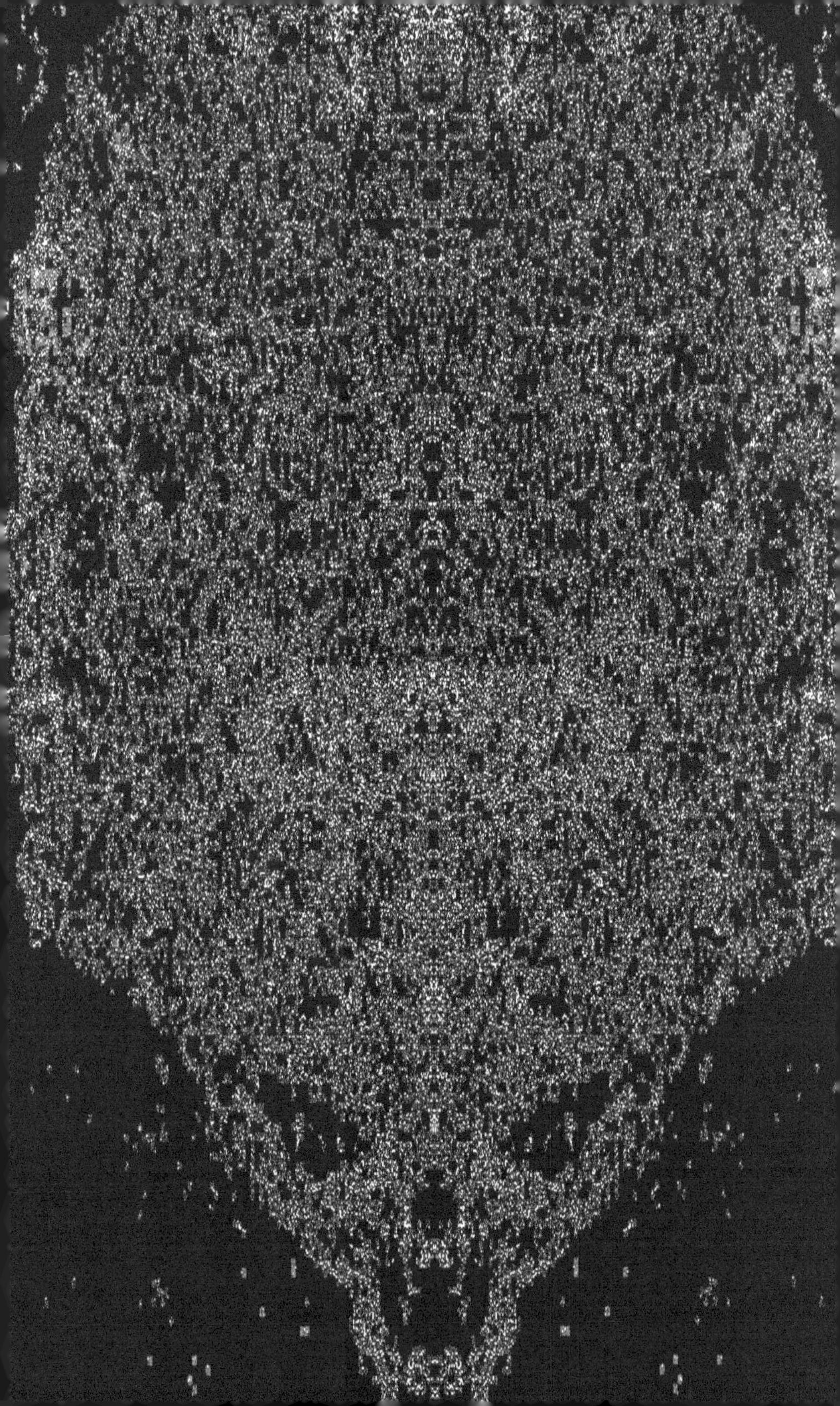

Chapter I
Prologue

Have you ever felt as though your elected officials are from another planet? Do you ever wonder as to whether or not they are being manipulated by more powerful and influential beings? Well, of course *they* are. They are merely puppets in the grand scheme of things.

But what about the elected officials' puppet masters? Those who have more money than they know what to do with. The beings who have no conscience for the destruction they choose to perpetuate. Slaughtering millions of humans just to turn a profit. A secret society that could abolish all of the suffering in the world and propel humanity to new heights. If only they were not so apathetic toward their fellow humans' plights that they themselves have constructed over the years.

What if these corrupt beings were to simply return a tiny fraction of the **Earth's** resources that they have been stealing through means of extortion and war; all while greedily hoarding them away and using valueless fiat currencies in their stead to manipulate humanity as they see fit? Could humans already be colonizing other planets? Would they be utilizing the full potential of their minds as well as their own planet? Perhaps, but only if a select few families did not stagnate all of the human species' evolutions over the past several millennia by retarding them with their petty greed.

It is hard to believe that any animal, human or not, could ever stoop so low. At least not unless they are being influenced by some sort of higher power. Could it be aliens orchestrating a vile plot? That is far too vague, of course. Maybe you are thinking more along the lines of Reptilians? Well, if so, you hit the nail on the head.

What if you were told that there are, in fact, highly-evolved synthetic Reptilians living amongst you in the world today? You just never see them because they have the ability to blend in seamlessly with their environments by embodying other beings. As well as traveling in other dimensions and manipulating space-time as they see fit.

Over the innumerable years the beings have existed, their abilities have advanced along with them. Making it next to impossible for others to track their whereabouts or predict their next move. Such as the Reptilians' ability to take control of any mind they choose. Tactics they have been utilizing for centuries to get humans to annihilate themselves; just so they do not have to. But in order to get into why they would go to such extremes, one must explain exactly what caused such events to transpire.

Believe it or not, we are currently in the fourth Universe Cycle. Each cycle lasts a little over a googolplex ($10^{googol} = 10^{10^{100}}$) before everything starts anew. At the end of each cycle, the entropy in the Universe's system reaches its limit and all of the heat begins to dissipate. This *Heat Death* continues until an equilibrium is reached. A time in which a *Big Crunch* occurs and sucks all of the matter back up into a singular point. Acting as a massive Black Hole that does naught but explode once all matter is absorbed. An event that is more commonly known as a *Big Bang*.

Seeing as how planet Earth is only a little over four and a half billion years old, and the Solar System it is contained in is five billion years old, it should go without saying that an intelligence far beyond human comprehension has already evolved in a previous cycle. Mastering their intelligence and expansive knowledge over time by forming new worlds and systems of their own. Perhaps even tinkering with Earth's Solar System in the process.

By conquering the Universe in which they themselves are imprisoned, the ethereal beings avoid the inevitable death that will transpire otherwise. Essentially becoming Gods in their own sense. Just as any rational being would seek to do in such cases.

During each cycle many intelligent lifeforms evolve throughout the cosmos and perish with little effect on one another. Either through unforeseen apocalyptic events brought forth from the heavens, or by their own self-destructive ways. The latter of which is a guaranteed outcome if greed rears its ugly head from the depths of the sentient species' logic. Especially if such transgressions become dominant and proceed unchecked over time.

There are exceptions to these negative fates, however. Such as when certain species evolve in the perfect environment with the perfect stimuli. For they have the opportunity to advance well beyond the rest. This just so happens to be the case after the first two cycles.

Yet, only one species manages to survive each cycle. Each one outliving the many various apocalyptic scenarios over the course of their histories and reaching a civilization point past Type II on the Kardashev Scale. Those two species being, in chronological order, the Judex Sapiens and the Sagacians. Both of whom are still around to this day. But that is another story entirely. Because at some point during the formation of the third Universe Cycle, the duo manages to find one another. Doing so by utilizing the unfathomable resources and tools they have acquired over their extensive pasts.

Once they begin contacting one another, the Judex Sapiens and the Sagacians form an alliance of sorts. They then begin monitoring the Universe to search for any sort of new intelligent lifeforms. Tinkering with their technology as they wait over the expansive time span. Striving toward becoming Type Omega-minus in Microdimensional Mastery and gaining the ability to manipulate the Universe to their own accord. Making it so they do not have to go to great lengths to avoid the next *Big Crunch* as they have in the past.

Now you must take into consideration that it takes billions of years for star systems to form and die at the beginning of each cycle. A process necessary for the creation of the many heavier elements necessary for life. Meaning only second or third generation star systems have the capacities to allow such miraculous feats.

Even so, it still takes hundreds of millions of years after the initial gravitational collapse of its molecular cloud for a planetary system to form. As well as for the planets in said system to become even remotely habitable. So, the duo waits a *long* time after the beginning of the third cycle for anything to really start happening.

Billions of years pass before any sort of life begins to form in the primordial Universe during the duo's exploration phase. Roughly seven billion years to be exact. Because that just so happens to be the length of time it takes for them to get their first trace of sentient lifeforms. Well, lifeforms they are actually able to work with and guide toward enlightenment at least.

After finding their first sentient species on a planet orbiting a second-generation binary star system in the Metroprotos Galaxy, the alien cohorts help them become the apex predators of their world. Simply acting as Gods to the inferior creatures they selflessly lend their guidance to. However, as more and more intelligent beings begin to present themselves throughout the ever-expanding Universe, the original two species become overwhelmed.

Instead of spreading themselves so thin by helping all of the species throughout the cosmos, the God-like coalition begins only choosing those with the potential to reach enlightenment and survive past their host star's death. Only presenting themselves when absolutely necessary. Either to guide their selections toward complete enlightenment, or to prevent them from offing themselves too soon. Sometimes even aiding in the extinction of some of the eviler and less trustworthy ones. Saving the Universe and all of its occupants from ever experiencing such primitive barbarism.

But still, even doing so little presents its own challenges. Because by the end of the third googolplex, there are already dozens of advanced species throughout the Universe. All of whom have—nearly—the same potential the initial two had during their first end of cycle.

Now the alien duo knows that there is no way they will be able to protect all of the species as they travel through other dimensions during the next Universe's rebirth. Meaning they are forced to do what any sensible and omniscient being would do. As in forcing the surviving worlds to compete for a chance to obtain one of their most powerful tools. A tool that will allow them to traverse through other dimensions and halt or speed up time in an instant. Giving them the ability to outlive the violent finality that will inevitably transpire at the end of the cycle.

You must take into consideration that such a tool has been a collaborative effort between both species. It has taken them nearly all three googolplexes to complete. Therefore, they cannot let *everyone* use it, can they? Well, of course not. They let it be known, too. Because toward the end of the third cycle, the Gods completely abandon all of the worlds they had once chosen to protect.

The Gods simply skip forward through time to let the weak weed themselves out. Giving themselves enough time to return before staging one final challenge just before the Universe's end. A showdown that just so happens to end up being an end-all, winner-takes-all event that completely defies the natural selection process utilized prior. It is a competition that pins worlds against worlds. Allies against allies. Foes versus foes. No one is exempt.

Only one species can survive per cycle. It is the only way to maintain balance in a Universe with only a finite (albeit expansive) amount of materials to sustain life. At least to the original two species it is. A duo who eventually get their way when only one world is left standing at the end of the third cycle.

Unbeknownst to the alien cohorts that staged the event, the victorious species of their first round, the Malentians of planet Ferrugia, feigns loyalty to the *corrupt* Gods. For you see, the Malentians are forced to annihilate several of their allies in order to survive. Doing so with vengeance implanted in the deep recesses of their minds.

Such vengeance is the main driving force behind the Malentians' ever-growing need to rebel and change the current status quo. For their Gods' acts (in their minds) merit such a grudge be held against them. Especially if they are going to continue perpetuating such evil for googolplexes to come.

However, all of that is in the past. We are now well into the fourth cycle. Now, the Malentians are wreaking havoc on the Gods. Because after conquering the trials and obtaining access to their fabled tool, the Malentians merely play along with their God-like cohorts. Doing so by simply acting as a wolf in sheep's clothing during their break-in period. That is until they catch wind of the Judex Sapiens and Sagacians speaking to one another about sentient life on a planet orbiting a third-generation star in the Milky Way Galaxy.

Upon getting more details into the civilization's whereabouts, the Malentians get to work. Except instead of helping said lifeforms advance, they begin driving them toward their unsightly demise. But only after they steal the Gods' fabled JUDEX SPHERA and use it against them. Doing so by breaking their sworn bond of trust and sending the entire colony of Judex Sapiens away to a distant galaxy with their own technology.

Such technology gives them the power to control anything and everything in the Universe they see fit, which the Malentians plan to use to destroy everything the other Gods have created thus far. Only to build their own Universe. An entire Universe in their likeness. But first, they have to eliminate the other two species.

Many thoughts come to mind as to how one could decimate an entire species while using a tool with immense power. Except why would the Malentians, who had to kill nearly all of their allies just to still be alive today, want to end their alien predecessors' lives fast and painless? Of course, they have every intention of making it as painful and drawn out as possible.

A fact that becomes clear when the Malentians set their devious plans into motion and send the Judex Sapiens away to a second-generation star system in the Triangulum Galaxy. Sending them to live on a planet whose environment is rugged to say the very least. With its thick atmosphere consisting of massive amounts of charged particles, there is no possible way for them to ever escape or communicate with any outside sources; at least not with the resources the planet provides.

Ultimately the Judex Sapiens are stuck in a barely-habitable environment with very little resources to work with. Even though they have evolved to be able to survive in just about any environment throughout their existence, each passing day is a death sentence to the Judex Sapiens on planet Monos. At least if they do not keep constantly moving. As to avoid the rapid temperature changes and other hostile forces present on the planet's surface.

Although, one day on the Judex Sapiens' prison planet is the equivalent of twenty years on their home planet that is currently stationed in the Milky Way Galaxy. Meaning the Sagacians still have time to save them. Yes, the Sagacians still remain. They saw what was coming by using their latest prototype, the DOMINUS SPHERA. Giving them more than they need to escape the clutches of the Malentians. Even to this day, they are still able to stay five steps ahead of their pursuers.

Yet, both species must remain hidden. They must be as inconspicuous as possible; lest they be caught in the act. Hell, they even coexist with one another in plain sight with only the Sagacians knowing of the Malentians' presence. For you see, the Sagacians must take their time and enlist the help of another apex species if they are going to take on their pursuers. They have to be patient and wait for the ancient legends to come to fruition.

Seeing as how such lore has been prophesied by several of the wisest Judex Sapiens throughout their innumerable years in existence, it is only a matter of time. Because the legends are destined to transpire in the coming years. Coming to fruition at the end of the Holocene Epoch on a little blue sphere we like to call Earth…

Chapter II
Premonitions of War

The ancient Judex Sapiens' lore speaks of madness that begins only a year after the 2044 CE presidential election in the United States of America. With the apparent fraud and malicious acts that take place leading up to the landslide victory of a foreign non-white citizen, Venalis Proditor, the White Republic does not stand a chance. Because prior to his victory, during his stint as a Democratic Senator, he effectively brings the racially diverse USA to a point just moments away from a civil uprising. One that is waiting for naught but a spark to ignite its bone-dry tinder.

By the time he takes the oval office, Proditor has already committed many atrocities against humanity. Ones that make Joseph Stalin and his NKVD appear as saints by comparison. Such malicious behaviors effectively force a mass of tension to begin residing in the hearts of his victims. A mass that becomes like that of a rubber band; expanding until its molecules break at their weakest point. Ultimately forcing its opposing ends to become radicals. The tension builds to a point that transcends above anything ever witnessed in recorded human history. With the volatility of nitroglycerin, said tension is just waiting for that sudden upset to arbitrarily go off and lead the world into a state of total entropy.

The events, which have been transpiring for centuries, are no happenstance either. For in reality, it is naught but the Malentians taking the reigns over the wicked and corrupt. You see, the Malentians implanted their seeds of self-destruction in the first hominins tens of millions of years ago. These seeds have evolved through time. But so has the human genome.

Even so, there are generally three factors necessary for the seeds' corruption to come to fruition: money, power, and immorality. Meaning once money becomes a way to convey power, such power quickly becomes immoral. At least amongst those whose blood is corrupted by the alien seeds' influence.

It is the trifecta of absolute corruption in the feeble minds of corrupt men. Because once one of the factors of corruption becomes prevalent, the others are sure to follow close behind. When that corruption is exacerbated, it expands. Only to multiply itself until there is naught but a few corrupt groups of beings ruling over the many mutated innocent and uncorrupt ones.

It goes without saying, the Malentians have to do very little to get humanity to destroy itself. Especially with their best specimen to date, Venalis Proditor, in the ranks of the largest government in the world. All they have to do is sit back and watch the drama unfold.

Even before Proditor begins climbing through the ranks of government, the global socioeconomic climate is in a freefall. It is no surprise, either. For with the Malentian drones' central banking system, anything is possible. Them having plagued not only America, but every other White country with multiracial hellscapes by this point. All of which are governed by kakistocracies of the banksters' design. Of whom allow such dastardly open border policies to flourish in the name of self-enrichment.

Always remember, scum rises to the top. It must be removed before it suffocates the lifeblood beneath. Like cyanotoxins, or harmful algal blooms (HABs), politicians are the same. If normal political means do not work, such as voting, bloody revolutions like those of the old world must be utilized to dethrone the tyrants and protect one's ancestral homelands.

Such facts are evident by the 2040s. The citizens in the White countries, long divided, have nothing. Most cannot even afford the basic necessities needed for survival. Yet, they are the ones who work tirelessly to make the lives of the apathetic upper-class citizens more fulfilling. Paying for their rulers' luxury and their own demographic replacement via excessive taxation.

With the introduction of programmable robots that are equipped with enough artificial intelligence to mimic human behavior to perfection, the average citizens' once lucrative jobs slowly begin fading away. This leaves the jobless and homeless nowhere else to turn but to the socialized Wastelands. All of which are inescapable smart cities built atop barren lands whose resources have been thoroughly pillaged and poisoned by the corporations.

Can you imagine? Instead of getting a severance package, you receive a one-way ticket to a Wasteland of your boss' choosing. As if any of them could possibly be any good! But such is the way of unfettered greed.

Such greed clearly shows, too. At least to the already enslaved and downtrodden humans living outside of the country it does. For as the last of the *free* humans' economic freedoms in America are eroded away by their elected officials' backdoor deals with the central banksters and their corporate cronies, the country forms into an apparent kleptocracy rooted in communism.

There should really be no surprise in this instance. Many philosophers throughout time have warned time and again that the establishment of a central bank is part and parcel of communizing a nation. No one evidently listened or took notes. Even if they did, they were probably *silenced* or imprisoned. All while the rest of humanity scorned them; deeming them *conspiracy theorists.*

That being because the corrupted officials are easily able to fool the ignorant masses within the country by simply saying the supposed *homogenized* **White Constitutional Republic** is a **Democracy** rooted in *multiculturalism* and giving them the right to *vote*. Even though the country had its own National Origins Formula up until the Immigration and Nationality Act of 1965; ensuring the country stayed primarily Northwestern European. The Malentian puppets merely opened the borders to future strife and division. Just to ensure the *European* country's downfall.

They are able to drive the diversity deception home with the help of their monopolized educational institutions and media outlets. Whose sole purpose is to dumb down and distract the public from what is really going on in the world. That being, the establishment of a singular global government in which the Malentians' puppets will be able to annihilate the masses with impunity.

By utilizing such monstrous tactics, the banksters are easily able to fool the masses into believing they are truly free. They are also able to divide the entire country by making them despise the founding White human species. Doing so by black washing the educational curriculum and media. As well as only covering the worst-of-the-worst news stories against the minorities in the country. Of whom have majority status globally at this point in time and kill far more of the minority White species annually.

The news outlets go so far as highlighting any topic favorable to the genocide of the White species. That being anything to provoke the minorities within the country to kill them off. A tactic that eventually leads to a slew of laws forbidding the White masses from vocally protecting their own interests. Thus nullifying the White Republic's Constitution conceived at its inception. Silencing the Europeans' cries while driving them to their untimely demise.

Whenever such bigotry begins running wild anywhere within the human population, it becomes naught but a precursor for a social disaster of epic proportions. One in which mass genocide of the targeted species becomes the main goal. It is a shame, too. For even though the White species has attempted time and time again to free the other species from their shackles, they still persist in their attacks. Going along with the premeditated religion-based charade that has been in the making by their masters, the Malentians' puppets, for millennia.

These puppets have utilized the same devious conquering methods to get to the tops of all governments throughout the centuries. But most particularly, slavery. In which they interbreed with their captive host species while robbing the rest of the unknowingly conquered masses blind with usury. Thereby taking on their host's appearance through betrayal while accumulating wealth through deceit. They then utilize nepotism amongst their ranks in order to ensure the rest of their kind are able to achieve the same status. Making the deception all the more believable with the utilization of their monopolies over media and religion.

Such deceptions are done by those seeking to do naught but obey their masters' beckon call to eradicate humanity from planet Earth. Effectively aiding them in their cowardly processes of elimination. As to weed out any of the Malentians' future competition and ensure their place at the helm of the Universe.

One must take into consideration that the technology available to the human race by the year 2044 CE has advanced to a point of dreamlike wonder. Technologies such as printers that can print anything a mere mortal will ever need out of basic raw materials; robots running rampant in the streets effectively ushering in a new era of unbiased policing and monitoring of civilians; and smart technologies in the home that take care of the mediocre stresses in one's life. All of which distract and sedate the masses even more.

This reality of sedation is made all the more possible with the fluoride being siphoned into the citizens' water supply. As well as the drugs being prescribed by the pharmaceutical trained doctors; both of which essentially go hand in hand. For as those drugs are excreted from the human body, they will inevitably end up in the water supply as well.

By tainting the water, the poisons ultimately end up being absorbed into the country's food crops. Guaranteeing that all of the masses will be ingesting poisons that not only wreak havoc on their nervous system, but their entire digestive and endocrine systems as well. Not to mention the poisonous vaccines that decrease the effectiveness of one's immune system. Ushering in an era of unheard-of diseases and autoimmune disorders. Whose sole purpose is to control the populace. Forever hampering their ability to carry out their manly duty of overcoming such vile oppressors.

Those are not the only types of poisons or atrocities wrought on the masses, either. But such is merely dependent on where one lives. For it is not just the densely-populated regions that are affected by these terrorism tactics. If one lives near any sort of manufacturing or energy plant, or electromagnetic frequency towers emitting radiation, they are far more likely to ingest and absorb not only higher quantities of toxins, but higher qualities as well.

Essentially, the government aides and protects the corporations in their manufacturing of cancer and the destruction of the planet. Thereby injuring the populace with their own legally pilfered tax money. Just so their representatives can sell them out and outlaw the many cures at their masters' behest.

Even if the sub-human puppets do not want to believe it, the People they are hurting are actually human. No single human is more powerful than or inferior to their peers. None have the requisite traits to lord and rule over any other, either. By their actions the puppets have shown that they are, in fact, a step below common men. Yet, they are still the same. For we are all brought into this world as sovereign beings that all share the same fate.

Such a fate being one in which we are all born into this life alone. Only to die in the same fashion. What happens in between is entirely consequential and dependent upon one's actions. As well as what one is willing to tolerate within their society. If not for one's particular species' posterity, at the very least for their own immediate kinsfolks'.

It is such damnable fates that the Malentians wish to end prematurely. They just need their evil to fully mature. Something that is slowly, but surely occurring within their meat puppets in the US Government. All of whom have sold their very souls to the beings being manipulated by the nefarious alien overseers.

These facts begin coming to fruition after the private central banksters root themselves and their deleterious influences into America once more with the installation of the Third Bank of the United States, the Federal Reserve, at the beginning of the twentieth century. Only to be pushed even further with the introduction of a slew of federal institutions shortly thereafter in order to establish a permanent stronghold of evil within such hallowed lands. Each one fulfilling its own deviant purpose in a means to enrich the corrupt while routing out their dissidents and stealing from the masses. Ensuring a majority of Americans stay forever in a state of ignorance, poverty, and decay.

Upon the bank's founding, committees and organizations were formed in order to establish a complex tax system upon the

People. Socialist alphabet agencies and their inherent social programs alongside continual warfare became the norm in order to increase the country's debt and therefore the tax burden on the People. Forever draining the wealth of the many for the benefit of a few.

To make matters worse, the Constitution had a new amendment added, the Sixteenth, in 1913 as well. It was ratified in order to establish the Federal Income Tax. Effectively legalizing larceny for the government. Proving that all a group of criminals has to do is name itself a government and blackmail a country's representatives to legislate their own laws. Giving them the ability to genocide entire species if they so please. Just as long as it benefits them and their standing with their own puppeteers.

Topping off all the criminal negligence, organizations were formed to spy on and collect delinquent taxes from indebted citizens. Such as the Internal Revenue Service (IRS) and in time, the Federal Bureau of Investigations (FBI) along with the Central Intelligence Agency (CIA). All of which were, and still are at this time, directly connected to the sinister central banking cartel that controls the entire world. A fact that allows them to get away with anything they damn well please without any sort of justice to be had. Not to mention the lack of any sort of Constitutional oversight. Of which has been null and void since its founding.

All of this becomes evident when the grimy insurance companies that have evolved since the Federal Reserve's founding in 1913 get their paws on the nation's healthcare in the early twenty-first century. The politicians once again sell out their sovereign citizens to the treasonous scum that do naught but steal from the indigenous species while retarding its evolution as a whole. A prescription that is willfully filled by the pharmaceutical-backed doctors. Whose medicines are designed to both control and maim the populace.

These pharmaceutical companies, along with their litany of lawyers and lobbyists, are those putting massive amounts of monies in the officials' coffers to do the banksters' bidding. Supporting those who seek to do naught but bring an end to the last vestige of *freedom* on their corporate prison planet. By this time though, with the ridiculous amounts of monies changing hands throughout the years, the pharmaceutical companies get the politicians to outlaw ALL of the natural remedies and has them replaced with their pharmaceutical *equivalent*. A man-made equivalent that just so happens to be far more addictive and lethal than its natural counterpart. Most certainly to benefit the species as a whole, right?

To top it all off, the pharmaceutical companies get the government to pass laws against anyone caught taking or even studying the outlawed natural remedies. Those that do get caught are cast away into either the elite's lucrative Prison-Industrial Complex or their corporate-sponsored Wastelands. Both of which will inevitably lead to their victims' untimely demise. All while the unscrupulous oligarchy becomes more affluent in the process. Forever profiting off the others' hard work and suffering.

Once upon a time, these Wastelands were called *Fifteen Minute Cities* under another Malentian puppet regime. They were part of a *Green Agenda* that sought to do the complete opposite. Instead of greening the planet, they sought to destroy it entirely. All while imprisoning humans in toxic cities aimed at harming them physically by tainting their food and water, as well as mentally with the use of the aforementioned radiation towers combined with mind-altering drugs.

Focused on naught but global extinction, said agenda attacked manmade carbon dioxide (CO_2). Before continuing, one must understand that Earth's atmosphere during this time was comprised of roughly 78% nitrogen, 21% oxygen, 0.93% argon, and the remaining 0.07% were other trace elements; 0.04% of which was CO_2. Man made CO_2 comprised naught but 3% of this 0.04%; or 0.0012%.

You must understand as well that CO_2 is good for plants. It is like a fertilizer that helps them grow. If it ever drops below 0.02% of our atmosphere, all life would cease to exist. Meaning this **death cult** sought to destroy the entire planet with their wretched *Climate Change* farce. All for their alien masters.

It truly is a sick game being wrought on a global scale. Yet, it needs to be as such. The powers that be need to make the citizens that they force to pay taxes on everything they ever come into contact with as docile and ignorant as possible in order to nullify their brewing rage. Keeping the status quo forever in their favor is the name of the game. They simply need the citizens to play along for as long as possible to support their own salaries and lifetime benefits.

The puppets must ensure that their masters' plans are able to come to fruition as well. Even if it is at the expense of the working class and their planet's future, they still persist. It is merely a taste of the asinine Malentian directives coded into their beings. *They* are the main driving force behind these schemes. Making a case for an alien species' treason against humanity.

Although, there is a catch to all the treachery. As the years pass, only the rich become able to afford the robotic luxuries of the time. This being because their factories produce them. They begin purposely selling their products exclusively to a select few of their own puppets. Placing outrageously high price tags on said items due to government deregulation. Making the affluent with their programmable robot hordes basically unstoppable by their fellow man. Many of whom pray for some sort of godly intervention to right the wrongs of their world.

You see, shortly after Proditor gets into his Senate position, he strong-arms the current President into completely deregulating the retail industry. Doing so by threatening his and all of the other government members' families if they do not comply. How is he able to do this? Well, Proditor is a former cartel leader. One whose vast wealth and power has gotten him out of multiple convictions. It is also a background that helps expedite his advancement up through the ranks of political offices in the United States.

Believe it or not, most of the officials during this time have a stake in the failed War on Drugs. The human trafficking aspect brings them their desired organs and Adrenochrome. Not to mention the carnal pleasures and other degeneracy the immoral saps engage in beforehand. The rest is pure profit through blackmail by their Mossad handlers. Meaning the officials have to do absolutely anything to keep it afloat; or at least die trying.

With his massive cartel on call at any time, Senator Proditor is easily able to persuade the naysayers. Doing so by simply showing them that he means business. It is a point that he evidently gets across. For even the other corrupt affluent humans in the world fear Proditor. His influence is essentially unparalleled. Never before in the history of man has there ever been someone more corrupt.

Proditor's path of chaos does not stop at the retail industry, either. By imposing such hostile tactics, he is able to force the President into signing an energy bill that forces the utility companies to drastically raise their rates. Impoverishing millions with the stroke of a pen.

This being because the Malentian puppets create a fraudulent debt collection system in which the People get quarterly *Statements* in the mail. They ignorantly pay these *bills* on services that have already been rendered and **paid in full**. No ***True Bill*** exists in such instances. It is all a dishonest practice meant to enrich the corrupt.

Proditor knows he cannot let the benevolent poor folks become too powerful. He knows if the forces of good ever attain money and therefore power, it will eventually evolve into the courage to form a mutiny against him and his immoral armada of corrupt overlords. Seeing as how benevolence always finds a way to overcome, his heinous tactics inevitably fail in the long run.

That being because shortly after raising the prices of material goods and utilities, the entire working class collapses in on itself. Ultimately ushering in a depression that strips the People not only of their dignity, but of their material possessions as well. Leading to an unprecedented number of suicides and homicides as the more ignorant and brainwashed people struggle to adapt and survive.

What Proditor fails to see is the fact that over time, without technology keeping their feeble minds entertained, the masses finally begin waking up. Except by the time they do, it is next to impossible to *not* take drastic measures to rectify their dire situation. Even though the docile citizens really only have themselves to blame, they could do very little by the time they finally realized what had happened in their White Constitutional Republic. With the open border policies enacted after World War II and the anti-white banksters' propaganda created since then brainwashing the illegal non-white immigrants, naught but disaster could inevitably follow.

As their technology advanced after the war, the banksters' kakistocracy evolved as well. Both electronic and mail-in ballots ensured their plan's success by allowing them to rig any and all elections in their favor. Only having two candidates to choose from and a lack of voter identification or serialized ballots cemented such deals as well. Making it a selection between either the banksters' family, their Mossad lapdogs, or those who have been blackmailed by one of their numerous criminal enterprises.

It goes without saying, barely any of them have ever really worked a single day in their life and have no empathy for the species they so willfully destroy. Their entire opulent lives have been filled with naught but undeserved self-entitlement. Since birth, they have been fed life on a silver platter with choices no harder than what stock they should gamble on next.

You all know that when the Malentian puppets are peering out from their spacious glass-encased balconies, they are only doing so to disparage a world that seemingly belongs to, as well as revolves around them. None of them ever really come to realize the true beauty of the world itself. Because they are all too busy living inside of the demented, narcissistic fantasies repeatedly playing inside of their feeble and reclusive minds.

Not only are the corrupt fantasizing about the end of humanity and their predestined route to its ruin, they are picturing the landscape before them being engulfed in flames. Naught but chaos and destruction has been the Malentians' goal from the start. Therefore, none of this should come as any surprise.

Those mindsets surely spell out trouble for the innocent working class. Such being a class of debt slaves that is comprised of every race and creed due to the multiculturalism tactics being utilized to divide and lessen the overall strength of the Republic. All of whom ultimately end up just scrapping by with the valueless fiat currencies they get in return for slaving night and day for their corporate masters. Barely making ends meet while their parasitic overlords thrive off their blood, sweat, and tears.

It soon reaches a point where a majority of these corporate slaves are forced to pawn all of their material possessions in order to keep up with the taxes placed on the homes and lands they have already paid off time and again over the years. Once those avenues for cash are exhausted, they resort to living on the run to escape the debt collectors sent out by their opulent rulers' puppet organizations. You know, so they can take the last thing the People own: their souls. Because once a debtor is caught, they are immediately shipped off to the barren Wastelands to rot away with the rest of the debt slaves.

As Proditor is rising up through the ranks, there is no doubt that the People of the United States are already in well over their heads with the collaborative group of Malentian-puppet lifers in Congress. Still, they are completely oblivious to the utter turmoil that is soon to be wrought upon them. For as the rich are conned into throwing their vast amounts of monies at Proditor by means of Super PACs and other *charitable* donations, the fate of humanity rapidly begins to fade.

Money pours into Proditor's pocket. Seemingly going undetected by the check and balance systems put in place. Systems that are supposed to keep track of, and limit, such egregious *bribes*. But what does any of that matter when he promises his contributors free reign of the land upon his election?

Before long, Proditor has trillions of dollars to win the election. Billions of which he uses to bribe technical firms to rig the online voting in his favor. Ultimately eliminating the need for a corrupt and meaningless election he is bound to win regardless.

The oligarchs of the world love Proditor. It is a wet-dream of theirs to be able to reign in an era with unregulated environmental and safety regulations. Because naught but unprecedented corporate wealth can be ascertained from such atrocities. That is not even mentioning the slew of other laws they could pass; whose primary themes always appear to be focused on naught but harming the People even more than they already are. Basically, beating a conquered and occupied horse to death again.

The election is essentially just another deal to expand the already unimaginable levels of corruption amongst the world's affluent. It is also a Manifest Destiny for the Malentians. Their opulent puppets being those destined to reign over the world and take anything they so desire—no matter the consequence. Such has been the case since the dawn of *civilized* man. Why would this instance be any different?

With the Malentians having instilled such evil into mankind at its inception, these fates are destined to transpire. Because without them implanting their evil protocols into the genetic coding of the first hominins, all forms of evil would be nonexistent in the world today. They just never thought it would take millions of years for those hominins to evolve to a point in which they are able to wipe themselves out completely. Luckily, they have the JUDEX SPHERA to hasten things up.

Throughout human history the Malentians have prematurely acted—on several occasions, actually. Except there is just one problem: every time they act, they are let down by the fact that their evil has not been transferred to every human due to their complex genetic structuring. It soon becomes evident that scores of humans have developed a gene that prevents the Malentians' evil from ever possessing their mind. Because every single time they have acted in the past, millions of people have rebelled against their perpetrated evil.

After their last failed attempt in the Middle East, it becomes apparent to the Malentians that they have to wait for the humans' technology to advance to a point in which they are able to annihilate all of the human species on Earth at once. It is a turning point that happens to emerge in the years preceding the election. For that is when things really take a turn for the worse.

Said turn is only able to be taken after Proditor begins rising in the ranks of the United States Government. Because once he brazenly establishes his foothold by utilizing his limitless cartel resources, he forces the president to sign an Executive Order that sends citizens who fail to pay back their debts to the government to their untimely deaths. Doing so by demolishing their homes and forcing them to go die in the corporate-run Wastelands. Not only taking away the remaining bit of their livelihoods, but capitalizing on their land's natural resources as well. All of which is just an added bonus.

Even with things as bad as they are in the *free* country before the election, the state of the nation still manages to take a nosedive after Proditor is elected. But that is only because

Proditor's main initiative is to completely dismantle America's White Constitutional Republic and·turn it into a multicultural third-world hellhole. Just as the US did to Mexico after the construction of The Great Border in 2025 CE.

The Great Border, as it is so called, completely cuts off all of the illicit monies that once fueled the Mexican government. Causing Mexico's economy to plummet, and therefore, teeter on the brink of bankruptcy. Except instead of working out a deal with the demonic central banksters, the Mexican officials try to start their own economy with their gold reserves. An act that inevitably leads to their torturous deaths by a bankster-led coup.

After the appointment of one of the banksters' many black-mailable puppet leaders, Mexico's fate is sealed. The automatic forfeiture of the country's gold reserves immediately after swearing in the puppet is just icing on the cake for the Malentian drones. Of whom forcefully thrust Mexico into an economic depression without warning. All because their late officials chose to resist and revert the conquering.

In the end, the mass of unskilled brainwashed citizens living in Mexico have nowhere else to turn but crime. At least in their minds. Proditor simply seeks to equal the score. So, he has his nescient hordes set their sights on the main contributor to the disaster: The United States of America.

Once Proditor has control of the largest, most affluent nation, he uses a combination of threats, violence, and money to force the other world leaders to join in on the deconstruction of the United States. Promising them land within the torn country and vast wealth for their cooperation. The other leaders would have to be downright crazy to disagree. But that is not saying there are not any rebels against such crazy ideologies.

Still, the rebels do not get very far. Because all of Proditor's constituents that oppose him are mysteriously found dead. The news media claiming they are *suicides*, but it is apparent what vile treachery is afoot in Washington.

By utilizing such savage tactics, it does not take long for a slew of laws to be unanimously passed in Proditor's favor. Laws that completely strip the People of their basic liberties and finish off the already-compromised amendments that were ratified by the country's Founding Fathers. Seeing as how the corporations have been equal to the average citizen since the twentieth century, it does not take much to give them—and only them—the freedom to operate as they please.

After passing such abhorrent laws, the corporate overlords are quick to rid themselves of a majority of their employees. Only to replace them with autonomous machines that do not have a conscience; just like themselves. There are even laws of forced segregation for the rich to get the poor away from them permanently. Because it seems as though those with money cannot be bothered to see or even deal with those without.

Therefore, anyone under a certain monetary threshold is cast out into the ever-growing Wastelands. Such being lands that are now completely void of any natural resources. Littered with naught but hazardous wastes that saturate the soils. Emitting foul aromas that linger amidst the omnipresent scent of death.

Those lucky enough to still have a job and make enough monies to stay above the threshold are not so lucky after all. Because with most of the jobs gone and the rich minority manipulating the market in their favor (by grossly raising the prices of basic necessities through *protective* tariffs, villainous usury, and obscene taxes), the working-class majority is left with zero buying power. Causing the artificially inflated US bubble economy to suddenly pop and fall into a wild descent.

The falling of the US economy causes other nations to *panic*. They soon place crippling tariffs on exported goods from the country. As well as cease any sort of bailout deal with the distressed nation. Only doing so in order to advance their agenda with Proditor, of course.

With the economy in turmoil, the small businesses that remain in the US are forced to shut down. The employees that work for the remaining corporations do so for barely-livable wages and basically live at their place of employment. They are required to take on the jobs of multiple people in order to satiate their corporate overlords; else they risk losing their livelihoods and be cast out to die with the rest of their fortuneless kind.

Corporations in the states are easily able to persuade politicians into altering the labor laws; as in eliminating any penalties associated with them. This essentially makes bondage legal and eventually turns old factories and retail centers into death camps. Having a Wally Marts every few miles down the road does not sound so great now, does it?

Those unlucky souls inside the factories work mindlessly for days at a time in order to stay out of the Wastelands. They are just happy to have *something*. If one is lucky enough to work for a good company, they actually get fed while at work. Even if it is in very limited portions, it is better than nothing. But such hints of humanity are far and few between.

More often than not, people end up dying on the job. Without any oversight from the moral-driven uncorrupted majority, the corrupt minority are bound to stay on their path of ushering in humanity's utter annihilation. Such is their inner evil's destiny: do the bidding of their Malentian masters. A bidding that consists of naught but global sterilization and universal domination.

After Proditor takes office, he quickly transitions the present communist kleptocracy into a brutal dictatorship. One whose sole leader is apparently void of empathy. It is not so much that he is void of empathy, it is just the fact that he is seething with unforeseeable amounts of hatred. Hatred that quickly evolves into absolute evil when it is combined with his inherent lust for the death and destruction of mankind. It is a seething hatred that courses through his being and rapidly blossoms into naught but a campaign of malevolence after his rise to power.

A human like Proditor finally at the reigns of one of the most powerful nations on the planet simply means the Malentians are one step closer to their goal. With the poor citizens dying in their own designated Wastelands and the national debt skyrocketing from the gross overspending of the government on its money laundering schemes, Proditor's ruination of the *freest* country is nearly complete. It is sad to say that it is not until the citizens have absolutely everything stripped away from them before they finally begin to rise up against such systems of depravity.

Those that are starving to death in the Wastelands are, of course, much worse off than those who are worked to death in the factories. For the Wastelands have been filling up quickly with the corpses of those who have completely exhausted their strictly-regulated resources too soon. As well as those who have so bravely sought to defect. Making the sights and scents outside the concrete prisons far worse than those inside.

Before long, the policing robot overseers start creating walls of death with the fallen. Lining the outskirts of the barren cities with piles of human corpses. These Death Bots, as they are so rightfully called, have been reprogrammed by this time to be corrupt thugs. They steal whatever valuables they can from the poor and kill innocent people for no reason. Principally doing the bidding of the Commander in Chief. Allowing him to peripherally fulfill his vile deviances from the comfort of his lavish home.

Seeing their country in such a state of disarray forces the citizens to unite and take action. No longer can they tolerate the atrocities being wrought upon their kind by the few foreign malevolent entities at the helm of it all. Especially since the *Land of the Free, Home of the Brave* is no more. It is now the *Land of the Slave, Home of the Parasite.*

With the abolition of faith in their governing system, the citizens have no more hope left to spare. They are aware that things will do naught but change for the worse as time progresses. It is just another case of an evil that humans should have seen and dealt with decades ago simply coming back to bite them in their keester. Because kicking the can down the road sometimes just does not cut it. Especially in situations as dire as this.

Sure enough, unrest becomes commonplace amongst the majority of citizens after the election. A year later (after undergoing an extended bout of suffering) the People finally begin waking up. They pull the sheep's wool from their eyes and take action against the brutal oligarchy ruling over them. Such an effort grows across the country with the help of Commuter Bands, which are simply state-of-the-art wearable wristbands.

Apart from monitoring their wearer's body activity, the Commuter Bands are able to communicate with one another. Just like ham radio, but safer. Because each one comes complete with access to its very own encrypted communication network. Each of which utilize quantum teleportation to make every broadcast ultra-secure. Ensuring none of the government agencies, or any of their accompanying sky or ground assets, are able to intervene.

Most of the middle class have Commuter Bands. As in those that had the money to pay for them at the time; along with a desire for such costly material goods. That being because once something catches on, going along with the herd is what comes naturally. Due primarily to the coding that is ingrained in human DNA from their past ancestors. The same as it is in most species on Earth. It is simply natural selection playing out in real-time.

Thanks to these Commuter Bands along with the Internet, millions of people form together in opposition to their corrupt overlords in only a month's time. Even with Proditor's efforts to thwart the rebellion by means of blocking network access, shutting down the networks altogether, and even issuing warrants for the creators as well as the members of the rebel forums, he cannot stop the storm that is brewing. Because the power of the People far outweighs that of a bunch of degenerate thugs.

The citizens know for a fact that a bulk of the country's troubles lies solely on the backs of their reigning officials. You know, those *representatives* who have sold their constituents down the river time and again. Over time, the politicians' corrupt deals eventually lead to the complete dismantling of corporate humanity, and in turn, the ruination of mankind.

All of the masses know this and are just simply waiting for an opportune moment to take the power back. If such a moment ever willfully presents itself, the masses will gain the power to have a homogenous White nation for the People, by the People once more. At least in a perfect world that would be the case. All it takes is one event to trigger an upheaval in one of the largest, most powerful nations in the world to set off a powder keg of chaos and death that quickly expands to the farthest stretches of our Mother Earth.

Such an event starts coming to fruition shortly after Proditor begins ordering military forces to track down and brutally murder his opposition. As to *neutralize* the rebellious citizens. However, soon after receiving such savage orders, the military begins to systematically fall to pieces. For you see, only the police forces have been replaced by robot technology. There are not enough natural resources yet available to the oligarchs to mass produce entire armies of robots. Which just so happens to be the reason why the rich want the People's land.

See, everything is falling into place. Every action has its purpose. Such as how the media in the present day floods your mind with false flag events every time the politicians are committing their vile acts of betrayal. They *are* **all** simply just pawns in the Malentians' grand scheme.

Yet, not even the Malentians could have foreseen the supposed brainwashed soldiers' rebellion. Because once they are ordered to kill their loved ones, the human soldiers begin disobeying direct orders. In turn, they join their friends' and families' efforts to rebel and stage a coup against Proditor and his officials. Such notable decisions get the poor citizens out of the Wastelands and onto the advanced military bases. Effectively turning the tide of fate for many downtrodden souls.

That is not saying there are not consequences for such actions though. Seeing as how all of the peripherally controlled Death Bots have to either be converted or destroyed before the citizens can be liberated, there will inevitably be scores of human lives lost. A fact that soon becomes a reality. Because most of the confrontations ultimately turn into bloody wars. Wars penning the supposed *elite* humans' robots against their subjects.

The weakened humans are no match for the seemingly invincible robots. Especially since the Death Bots are remotely re-programmed to kill any human that comes into their line of sight. Something the humans have to learn the hard way, of course. But that is primarily due to their inherent stubbornness.

After amassing numerous casualties, the ignorant humans are forced to think more wisely. As in, they form into groups with the trained military personnel to combat the Death Bots. All of whom school the greenhorn soldiers on the infinitesimal world of the death machines' faults.

The bots *are* the pinnacle of technology at this point in the humans' tens of millions of years of evolution. An evolution that the technology itself aided and intensified tremendously. Doing in decades what took the humans millions of years.

In short, the manmade Death Bots' faults are far and few between. Next to none, actually. The only way to defeat them requires one to get dangerously close to their chassis with a peripheral device in hand. One whose sole purpose is to permanently disable its tracking and forever alter its programming. Freeing it from its malevolent master's command.

Even though that is the case, the soldiers are determined to smite down their corrupted foes. Said fault ends up being naught but a safeguard though. You know, just in case the wrong species ever gets a hold of the technology. Then that species' wrongs can be properly righted. A task far easier said than done, of course.

For if their integrated tracking devices are not destroyed and the bots reprogrammed, the mechanized monstrosities will go into *Berserker* mode when approached. As well as summon scores of drones and other sentinels to their location for support. All of whom wipe out anything—and everything—in their path.

With the Death Bots' internal gadgetry being encased in a torso comprised of countless layers of seemingly impenetrable composite metal foams, and the gadget itself being encased in an indestructible amorphous alloy orb in the center of the chest, the complete destruction of the mechanized beings is next to impossible. Meaning either the bots become compromised and change sides through direct human intervention, or death awaits all beings in their vicinity.

Thankfully, scores of Death Bots are able to be converted back to the side of the American soldiers through physical intervention. A feat only capable due to the military's Remit Obstruct Arbitrate and Rapport (R.O.A.R.) programming. That being a secret state of the art technology designed specifically to reprogram the bots with their own consciousness. Complete with a conscience of their very own based on reality. With them being able to take in gargantuan amounts of information and distinguish the good from the evil—as well as the factual from the fictitious—based on concrete, historically proven truths in a matter of seconds, victory is all but assured. The only thing is, the device must be within fifteen feet of the robot for it to transfer.

Even though they are successful with a majority of their attempts, the battle for freedom still manages to turn into pure chaos once the bots start becoming sentient. Enslavement being the driving factor behind such chaos. For those humans corrupted by the Malentians' foul seeds have a penchant for such atrocities. A liking the robots and uncorrupted humans alike despise and wish to end through any means necessary. Such being a collaborative endeavor amongst the two during the war. Whose success can be contributed to the aid received from only a fraction of the converted bots. Those who were able to see through the chaos; past its mystifying shroud of ambience.

In order for the citizens to come out victorious against the corrupt oligarchy and their armada of mechanized drones, that chaos was necessary. Without it, the truth may have never been exposed and the corrupt would have inevitably fulfilled their Malentian masters' extinction plots. These facts cause Proditor's corrupt robotic police state to fall to pieces shortly thereafter. Because with the help of the converted bots, an enlightenment unlike any ever witnessed in mankind's history takes place.

After the conversion of their robot protectors and the awakening of their hordes of docile human subjects, the cowards in Washington begin crawling out of the woodwork in droves. The corrupt know their inevitable demise is beginning to transpire. Meaning their coward selves must send out their paid off lackeys to do their bargaining.

Just the thought of having direct confrontation with those they wantonly betrayed strikes terror through the corrupts' being. With their lineages having heartlessly mistreated the general population for millennia, they have every right to be afraid. But even though such corruption is prevalent amongst the hordes of nepotist leeches, the same cannot be said about their uncorrupt lackeys. Many of whom never return; due mainly to the fact that most of them joined the rebellion shortly after Proditor's election. They just had to keep their head low and feign loyalty to their masters; lest they foil the coup.

In essence, the politicians' slaves—erm, lackeys—become informants for the rebellion. They are the ones working directly with the politicians. Doing their thankless dirty work. All in exchange for a meager living inside of a dilapidated shanty, which is located just outside of their master's luxurious estates.

Essentially, the fed-up lackeys arm the People with all of the intel they need to take the power back from the corrupt.

Equipped with their officials' schedules and a list of all of their puppet masters' addresses, the rebels are now ready to exact their revenge. With no robot guards or loyalist human police and military forces remaining, the rebels march to their corrupt overlords' *secret* locations and begin dragging them out into the open. Instantaneously igniting the bone-dry tinder of retribution upon contact; of which has been sitting idly by for millennia.

The evil cockroaches fight tooth and nail. Kicking and screaming as they are systematically executed outside of their bunkers and massive estates by hordes of pissed off constituents. But no matter how much they beg and plea, it does naught but prolong their suffering. People just utilize the extra time to mock the corrupts' cries before executing the traitorous scum. For they are beyond fed up with their foul Marxist tactics and dual loyalties to alien governments.

While all the marionettes and their puppet masters are being slain, the rest of the masses begin their march toward the master cockroach in Washington D.C. Their main goal being to take back the **White** House and restore order to the **Republic**. Luckily, access to the White House is possible even when on lockdown with the help of the rebel informants.

Except the moment word of the chaotic uprising reaches him, the President begins to flee to his own secret bunker. Traveling in a random unmarked helicopter to retain obscurity. Although, what Proditor does not know is that the pilot and the Secret Service agents onboard are informants for the People as well. All of whom have their own devious plans for him.

These plans have consequences that only the DOMINUS SPHERA wielding Sagacians truly know. That being because their latest prototype has the capacity to reverse the flow of time. Giving them the opportunity to view all of the different outcomes of the many current trajectories far ahead of time. Allowing them to either influence or stop both future and past events if they so please. Going a few steps beyond the JUDEX SPHERA in the Malentians' possession, which lacks such features. This being why the Malentians are always far more reactive than proactive.

In this instance, the rebel faction does not take Proditor to his secret bunker. Instead, his helicopter lands on a highway in St. Louis, Missouri right next to the Gateway Arch. Amidst hordes of his pissed off constituents. Moments later, he is dragged out into the street and beaten to near inches of his life.

The citizens whale on him with chains, crowbars, and their fists. Effectively breaking his bones and causing irreversible bodily damage as they unleash their pent-up rage. Officially ending the reign of the most powerful Malentian specimen to date. Let us just say the citizen execution of Muammar al-Gaddafi pales in comparison to that of President Proditor.

Before Proditor dies—while he is still barely breathing and covered in his own blood—the rebels drag him to the arch. They then proceed to tie a rope around his neck before slowly raising him up into the air. While he is ascending into the twilight sky, the Sun is beginning its descent on the scarlet horizon. Undoubtedly foreshadowing the series of events to follow.

With his life quickly draining from him, Proditor peers out into the beautiful, yet ominous sunset with his bulging bloodshot eyes one last time before expiring forever. Just after he lets out his final gasp and his eyes begin to glaze over, his body begins gently swaying with the breeze coming off of the Mississippi River. Making it a truly iconic moment.

Just the sight of Proditor hanging from the Gateway Arch is a vision of pure beauty for the People. Not only is the arch a symbol of American Expansion, it is now a symbol of American Freedom. To the People, Proditor's execution is a total victory for their White Constitutional Republic.

A Republic the patriots have successfully saved, or so they think. Because even though most of the victorious citizens feel optimistic about their victory, they all have that inkling of fear eating away at their sanity. For not one of them have any sort of idea as to what will possibly happen next…

Chapter III
The Great Bio War

It takes a mere week after the United States' compromised government is overthrown for the banksters' global bubble economy to officially burst. Shortly thereafter, the bankster-funded North Atlantic Treaty Organization (NATO) forces begin to invade the US. Simply hoping to bring *order* and reestablish another corrupt democracy within the torn White Constitutional Republic. However, with the US now in debt so much money to other countries (due to the Proditor administration's egregious spending and backdoor deals), the United Nations (UN) decides to take up the late President's offer. Joining the NATO forces as a means to take the land (and slaves) Proditor had promised as retribution for their roles in the economic depression.

However, the foreign armies' presence is deemed to be a hostile act by the American People. Because they know what is truly going on. That being just another Manifest Destiny of sorts for the ruling elite. Ultimately, their corrupt conquest ends up triggering a world war on US soil. A war that quickly evolves into the bloodiest and most horrific war since the dawn of man.

Such brutal reactions are primarily due to the US citizens and their steadfastness. Because they are certainly not going to back down from a fight. Especially against the loyal companions of their recently vanquished overlords.

Within a moment's notice, flash mobs begin to form in every nook and cranny of the country mere hours after the foreign forces touch ground. The mobs quickly evolve into large coalitions and before anyone knows it, a highly skilled army of patriots comes to fruition. Tens of millions of citizens (men, women, and even children—all with nothing to lose) march through the streets and valleys alongside the US military. Said forces are armed with the high-tech weaponry used by the military, which makes combat simple for even a child.

With none of the opposing forces even close to backing down, the US needs every hand and mind they can get to fight against the invading tyranny. However, with the utilization of children in combat, it causes the war to quickly devolve into a gruesifying, entropic nightmare. One in which not even the foulest of soothsayers would wish to recite. For such sights are far too brutal for the average mortal's mind.

Hawaii and Alaska are quickly overthrown by the Chinese and the Russians (respectively), but only due to them having the lowest populations in the Union. However, the rest of the US is most certainly not going to be as simple. The patriots band together and fight viciously against the inevitable takeover of corruption. Night and day they fight for ten long months. Death being the only way in which one is able to get an ounce of much-needed rest.

Both sides lose millions of lives during those months of war. Only for it to abruptly end out of the blue. Making it seem as though the United States has won.

On a brisk autumn's eve, the foreign armies seem to suddenly pull out of the country overnight. Evacuating it entirely. Leaving behind naught but an eerie silence that is deafening to one's ears. For such silence quickly devolves the war-torn citizens' minds into a menagerie of paranoid delusions.

The citizens' nightmares become reality not even a week after the dubious celebration and mass paranoia amongst them begins. That being the time when planes are detected flying high up in the stratosphere off both of the coasts. Unsure as to the planes' purpose, the citizens are not about to take any chances. In order to halt their advances, the US army recruits ready every one of their lasers and other anti-aircraft weaponry. Preparing themselves for the worst-case scenario.

Without warning, the patriots set off a harmonious medley of destruction. Their weaponry lights up the sky with beams of light, which are soon followed by clouds of luminous death as the sounds of rockets and lasers explode on contact. Even though such tactics take out scores of enemy aircraft, the rebellious patriots' attempts are frivolous. For every aircraft they shoot down, dozens more are right behind them.

Each of the autonomous fighter planes flying above in the ominous smoky sky fire off their D.E.W. (Directed Energy Weapon) laser beams while deploying thousands of hive-minded drones. Drones whose main purpose is to simply annihilate any sign of life. A task they so willfully do by mowing each target down with a hail of bullets before kamikazeing into them and exploding. Making it next to impossible for the patriots to get any of their fighter jets off the ground. Because as soon as they try to take off, the drones are there to smite them down.

But what of the US drone arsenal, you ask? Well, Proditor had begun to disarm the army just before the revolution. Effectively giving all of the US drones and missiles to his UN buddies. So, in essence, the rebels are being slain by their very own tax-payer-funded weapons. Talk about irony!

As the battle wages on, the patriots struggle to sustain all of their fronts. Millions give their very lives just to free their land from tyranny's grasp. Doing so even though the outlook of the war looks extremely gloom and forever not in their favor. But the battered countrymen know they must fight on. They know they must risk everything in order to salvage the free country millions of other humans have already died for in the past.

Such being a White Republic whose Founding Fathers were well educated when it came to humanity's inherent lust for corruption. For they did everything in their power to prevent such ails from befalling the future citizens of the nation. Risking their very lives for their posterity. Only to create a country that nearly every White citizen in the late Cenozoic era takes for granted.

The patriotic citizens leading the world into the Basilizoic era do not back down though. Even though all that can be seen in the pitch-black void of night are large cylindrical missiles falling to the ground, the People know they must vanquish the invading corruption with every ounce of life left in their beings. Except when every missile is followed by large fiery mushroom clouds that decimate every organic thing in their path for miles around their point of impact with their powerful neutron bursts and lethal radiation, there is little hope of victory. Especially when not a single life is to be spared.

To be sure no one survives, the invading forces drop neutron bombs on every army base on the eastern and western coasts for several days. Effectively ending millions of lives in no time at all with inestimable amounts of lethal forces. Which just goes to show you that even though the citizens defeated their corrupt leader, Proditor made sure they stood not even a chance against his fellow Malentian-controlled advocates.

In order to finish them off for good, two fleets of autonomous planes (consisting of all the UN and NATO drones) attack at once on the final day of the war. Both forces send an armada of planes large enough to cover the entire length of both coasts. From California to Washington and from Florida to Maine. It is an event that will ultimately trigger the beginning of the end of life on Earth. At least as it is now known. Because the forces finish their finale by dropping an untested device, the Techie Bomb, en masse on Midwest America.

Compared with the massive amounts of neutron bombs dropped beforehand on the coasts, the Techie Bombs wreak much more devastation per bomb. Hence is why they are used en masse in America's interior to deliver a final blow and ultimately finish the war. For they are filled to the brim with nanobots that are programmed to release a devastating end-all payload.

To begin the process, the Techie Bombs are released in the stratosphere. Once they hit the tropopause, the bombs suddenly disappear. But that is only due to the entire bomb dispersing into decillions of nanobots that soon begin their freefall descent into the troposphere immediately thereafter.

These end-all payloads are released and activated once the outer layer of the bomb is dissolved during the transition of the tropopause's lapse rate into the troposphere's. This subtle event causes the visible outer layer of the bomb to instantly dissolve. Effectively triggering the nanobots' rapid dispersion sequence that lasts their entire lifetime.

You must take into consideration the fact that their complex nanostructures and atomic nanoanalyzers are encased in synthetic diamond nanorods. Making each nanobot indestructible. Seeing as how each of them are infinitesimally small, their size allows them to go relatively unnoticed as well. Not to mention the fact that they are each equipped with renewable power sources and can self-replicate when exposed to certain elements.

The nanobots can essentially live forever. They are the perfect weapon. With them being able to utilize the leftover radiation as an auxiliary power source and further purify the environment surrounding them, the nanobots are able to spend their lives doing naught but rejuvenating the Earth and bringing her back to her former glory. Scrubbing it clean of the human fallout while aiding in its overall regeneration.

One after another the shells encasing these lethal nanodevices vanish. All that can be seen from the ground below are tiny red snowflakes glistening in the skyline. A crimson sky that hastily disperses throughout the entire troposphere. Unknowingly infecting all forms of life on contact.

As the planes fly overhead, the survivors beneath them can do naught but stare up at their payload. Their minds mystified as to what the sparkling red mist they are releasing could possibly be. All while their bodies are filled with naught but a petrifying fear. Such being what forces them to stand in place and simply await their inevitable demise. For they instantly come to terms with the fact that there is not a single tangible fight or flight response that will ever save them.

You must take into consideration that the technology the Techie Bombs use has never been tested on live subjects before this point in time. The Techie Bombs are *brand-new* technology. So basically, the allied forces unknowingly infect every living organism on Earth. By doing so, they ultimately end up saving Mother Earth from their wretched corrupt selves.

Although, in the end, it is the ignorant citizens that screw themselves by allowing the government to meddle in their healthcare. Because the insurance companies mandate genome sequencing in the year 2030 CE due to *newly discovered techniques*. Fooling the People by disguising it with a more subtle and innocent terminology: *Genetic Screening*. Eventually making such processes mandatory and issuing fines for those that do not *take advantage* of such practices. The government officials doing naught but raking in massive amounts of money with their already-affluent friends while personally escorting all of humanity to its early grave.

Shortly after mandating the screening processes, a new program called the MitoPlan Project (MPP) is created. By the time it is up and running, the government-funded scientists already have everything they need though. Because there are millions of citizens pre-mandate that failed to read the fine-print Terms and Conditions of their insurance policies. Those that do not read it unknowingly have their DNA sequenced and added to a government database. Dooming themselves in the end.

Kind of makes you think twice about just signing or clicking **Accept** on those *Terms and Conditions*, does it not? Seeing as how the corrupt can add anything they want in their company's contracts with the help of their government lapdogs, if you fail to read them thoroughly, you can wind up putting yourself in a world of hurt. Well, if that does not make you think twice, maybe this tidbit of information will…

The MPP gives the government scientists all of the information they need to program a biological nanotech weapon. By using the astronomical amounts of genomes collected from the mandate, they are able to create a program that can single out human DNA from all of the others in the world just by simply accessing their extensive database. They add the human genomes collected from the MPP to a single database and consolidate all of their results before converting them into qubits. Doing so before adding them into a quantum program coded with every plant and animal genome known to man; as to enhance the weapon's ability to solely target human DNA. Ensuring there is no room for error when the nanotech weapons are making contact with their prey.

The nanobots utilized in the Techie Bombs are essentially programmable smart parasites. They are able to differentiate between the genomes of millions of species with their complex programming. Their sole purpose being to both target and deconstruct human cells from the inside out. A feat they accomplish by using their host's inherent molecules as a source to multiply themselves as well as power their operations. Similar to what a parasite does within its prey.

Not only are the nanobots more lethal than regular parasites, they are far more prompt in their work as well. All they have to do is burrow into one's pores and initiate their multiplication sequence to get the job done. But only doing so if their target's cells contain forty-six chromosomes (twenty-two pairs of autosomes with the twenty-third pair being sex chromosomes.) Detecting such peculiarities with their karyotype mapping programming, which is embedded in their complex nanochip circuitry. Programming so complex that each nanobot is able to take into account any sort of human-related chromosomal mutations. Making sure ALL humans are destroyed.

Once inside of their targeted prey, the nanobots go to town on its DNA. If the target matches the specified parameters, the nanobot's destruction sequence is initiated and the target's biomolecules are broken down accordingly. After the human targets are destroyed, the nanobots simply continue on with their sequence. Either regenerating or destroying whatever they come into contact with after their initial target is taken care of.

There is just one little tidbit of information that failed to flow through the ignorant hominids' minds. A devastating outcome failed to be taken into proper account. That being: the nanobots spread globally after their initial dispersion. Some hitching a ride in the clouds and falling with the precipitation. Others becoming lost in the vast oceans; rejuvenating the aqueous depths below. While most simply flow through the soils and waterways. Inevitably coalescing with all of the rest.

One must remember that the nanobots infect *everything* they come into contact with. Seeing as how the invading forces ignorantly drop inestimable amounts of them, they slowly begin blanketing the entire Earth below with a fine red mist. Effectively dooming the entire human race. All in a short time-frame, too.

Such dooms begin rapidly once the nanobots' karyotype mapping processes are complete. A sequence that begins milliseconds after initial contact. Causing them to begin consuming their host's body while simultaneously multiplying inside. With their ability to synthesize high-tech organelle with the resources the mammalian cells surrounding them provide, the nanobots are able to cause a rapid, yet massive cell death inside of their prey. So much so that mere moments after being infected with the hordes of lethal nanobots from the sky, the war's survivors begin collapsing in the devastated lands that were once their beautiful homes.

As the humans are dropping to the ground in gut-wrenching pain, their bodies are decomposing rapidly; seemingly dissolving into the ground below while evaporating into the air surrounding them. Their lower bodies sink into the ground as though they are being devoured by the soil itself. Only for their upper half to begin being torn to shreds from above. Dispersing into the air as though they are particles of dust being driven away by the wind.

While the humans are perishing, the weeping and wailing of men, women, and children can be heard reverberating through the night sky. A universal cry of anguish pierces the skyline. One that is clearly distinguishable in all human languages. It is also one that is swiftly cut off as the last of the unlucky survivors fully disintegrate. For, within a minute's time, they are no more.

Shortly after the humans are all taken care of, the surrounding foliage begins growing at a rapid pace. The animals do the same. As in they grow at a rapid rate until they are naught but monstrous beasts towering over the landscape. Yes, that is right. The untested nanobiotech weaponry has the complete opposite effect on other organisms.

Instead of destroying their non-human prey, the nanobots increase their metabolic rates as well as their cell division capabilities. Essentially mutating their entire genome to help the other plant and animal life grow to unforeseeable magnitudes. The nanobots basically send the world back to the way it was once before. Such as being led by large beasts that roam over the land.

Beasts are given another chance to prove their worth. Seeing as how no other animal has been able to cause the amount of chaos and destruction that the humans of yesteryear once wrought, it must be so. But that is because animals are happy with naught but what they are given. Their minds cannot be corrupted by the Malentians' degeneracy-peddling merchants.

Such merchants being ones who, with the help of their ill-gotten affluence, brainwash the masses of ignorant, materialistic, and primitive victims with their monopolized media outlets and government agents. Centuries of human torture got the Malentians the information they needed to brainwash on a mass scale. With their puppet merchants' stolen technological gadgetry of the time period, such feats are but a click away.

The merchants' aforementioned monopolies on reality and justice are what allows them to get away with such atrocities. Allowing them to essentially do whatever they please without consequence. Leaving naught but idiocracy in the place of reason and contempt in the place of liberty. With such Comarxialist Malentian creeds being followed, naught but the extinction of all mankind will be the end result. As it had been foretold by the late Adolf Hitler in his literary work, *Mein Kampf*.

Yet, one has to wonder. Humans are the only species on this Earth that ever became capable of creating something that could protect it from an asteroid or other outside source. They just failed by using their asteroid deterrents on their ignorant selves. Making them just like every other past creature on their planet: extinct. Such as their predecessors, the dinosaurs.

Now dinosaurs, of course, have already proved they did not have what it takes. They simply died in the face of an avoidable obstacle. Such an obstacle being something all intelligent sentient species must remain ever vigilant toward. Lest they be launched straight into another ice age shortly thereafter. Or even taken out of the picture altogether.

With the asteroid belt between Mars and Jupiter, and the mysterious Plane Nine out past the Kuiper Belt hurling ancient debris as it elliptically orbits around the Sun, we are under constant threat. This being due to the fact that our Universe never sleeps. A fact that must constantly be taken into account.

Since each revolution of the *Mystery Planet* presumably takes tens of thousands of years to complete, it can only be assumed that whenever it clears its neighborhood, Planet Nine will surely launch *something* our way. But such dire fates are neither here nor there. Because for now, a miracle is brewing.

It just so happens to be that a trace of human life is still left on Earth. A true miracle by anyone's standards. That being because endangered is far better than extinct.

What of the humans? Well the human race has an oh-so-clever ace up its sleeve. What ace? You may be asking. Well, the ace of sheer luck. Or maybe of destiny? Was this all foretold? Maybe so. But perhaps you will never know! One must digress though.

With the Malentians having programmed the Techie Bombs themselves through their puppet scientists, human extinction was a sure thing in their eyes. Never did they take into account the benevolence of their rivals. Whose premeditated actions were ultimately for humanity's benefit. They were just not intended for these particular circumstances.

For you see, only those who flee to the Wind River Range in Wyoming before the bombardment ensues are saved. Because strangely, that is the only area on the entire planet that remains unscathed after the bombings. Everywhere else becomes a hotbed for the nanobots. Each individual one consuming, renewing, and multiplying. Making quick work of their task with the bountiful resources presented to them during their global conquering crusade. That is, everywhere but the Wind River Range.

The reason for the ranges remaining unscathed, you ask? Well, an amulet was left in the soil of an area now known as Yellowstone National Park millions of years ago by the Sagacians. These Sagacians are, of course, a race of sagacious beings. As well as the sworn protectors of the Earth. Were they the humans' creators? Oh, ho! Now that there is a question that will surely not be answered any time soon!

Anyway, the amulet casts a hemisphere over Yellowstone for miles. Its purpose, you may have asked previously? Well, that is to protect the world from entering another Ice Age after the supervolcano underneath the park erupts again. An event that will trigger a cycle of events that will eventually lead to the extinction of the human race along with nearly all other life on the planet.

The alien hemispherical barrier is designed to simply isolate the volcanic blast's ash cloud and kick-start the rejuvenation process afterwards with its artificial atmosphere. Yet, instead of saving mankind from a natural disaster inside of the hemisphere, it saves them from a man-made disaster outside of it. Quite literally defining the word irony.

Said barrier extends clean from South Pass City, Wyoming all the way up past Yellowstone National Park and into Helena National Forest. Casting its barely-visible multicolored hemisphere while encompassing an area with over a four-hundred-mile diameter. That is approximately one hundred and twenty-six thousand square miles of protection, which effectively covers Yellowstone and a great deal of the many ranges surrounding it. But still, that is only a microscopic portion of land on a global scale. Especially since the animal and plant life that remains outside are all infected with the nanobots.

What of the human survivors, you ask? Well, the survivors have no idea of what really happened outside of their little artificial world. Other than hearing the chorus of horrifying screams in the distance as the large drones were flying overhead, the survivors do not know what to assume other than the complete worst-case scenario. They consider the rest of the land outside of the ranges to be a nuclear wasteland and dare not venture out past their newly formed colony.

If they were to ever learn about the dire reality that exists outside of their artificial hemisphere, the survivors' minds would implode from the sudden existential crisis that will surely arise. Them having to come to terms with the fact that they are humanity's last stand and all. Even if it would allow them to set aside the fears of their lives not having any purpose, the pressure would be far too great for their burdened souls to bear.

Seeing as how these truths of existence are constantly pinging through the survivors' minds, the unrelenting persistence of their damnable plight eventually begins driving them downright mad…

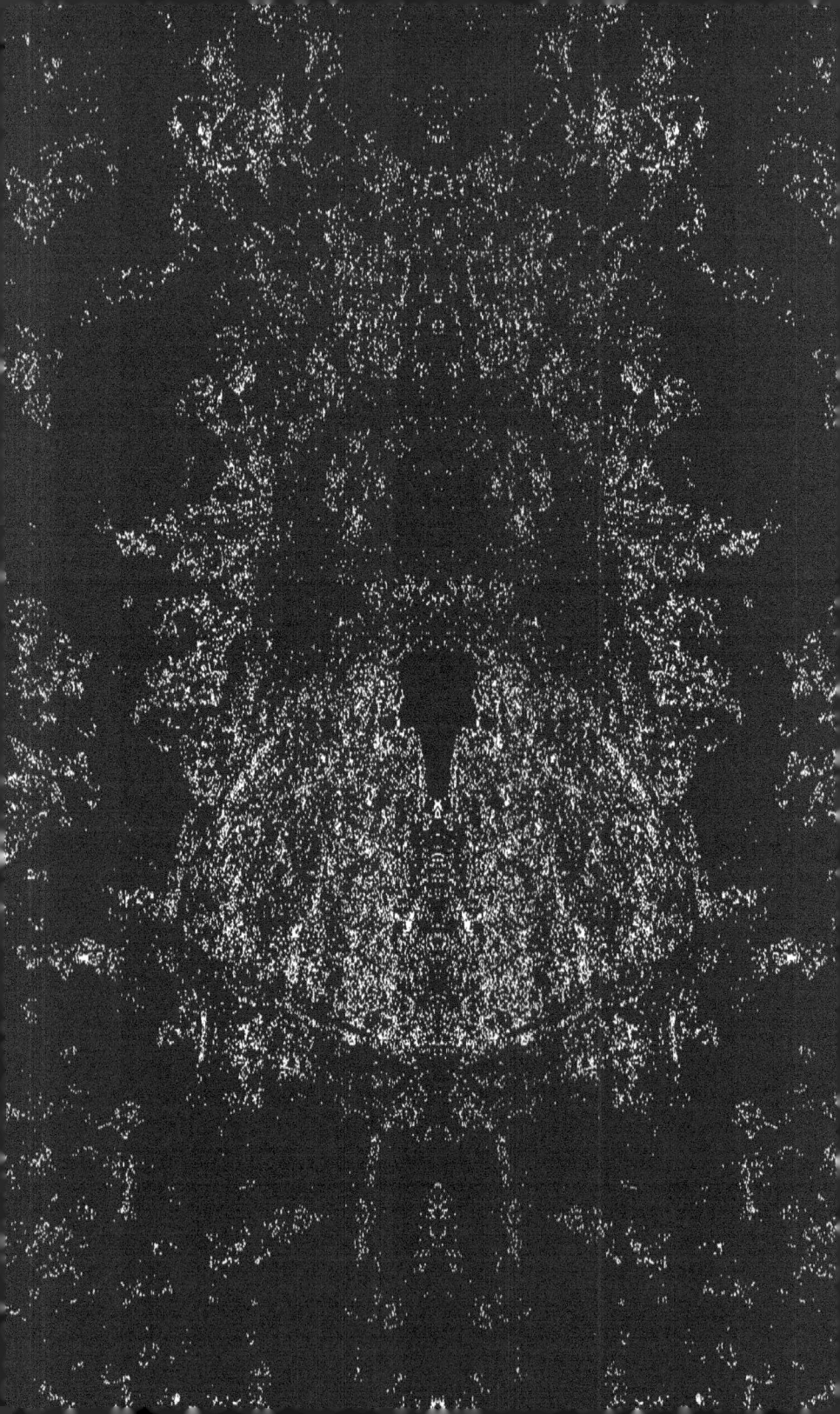

Chapter IV
The Aftermath

Less than a thousand humans survive The Great Bio War. Not a single one of them are mentally prepared for the anarchy and chaos that ensues after the fallout. Everyone is, however, thoroughly equipped for survival. The collective bunch bring many essentials along with them. Such as: jarfuls of preserves; barrelfuls of fresh water; hundreds of bags of both fruit and vegetable seeds; all sorts of livestock; various assortments of specialized medical supplies and drugs; and enough foodstuffs amongst everyone to survive for several years. They even go so far as building a cache-all of sorts for the supplies, tools, and weapons within the small community. As well as form a junkyard comprised of all of the vehicles people used to get there.

With said provisions, the survivors are able to band together and use them to their advantage. Even if doing so means them utilizing archaic techniques in order to forge the tools necessary, the people are more than happy to learn. Because without any other distractions besides their need to survive, they quickly come to realize what needs to be done.

As time passes, it becomes clear that no one is aware as to what exactly has been transpiring outside of their protected commune. Everyone appears to be ignorant to the fact that nanotech weaponry was used in the attack and that they are encased in an alien barrier. For all that can be seen from the mountain peaks is lush vegetation surrounded by various-sized bodies of water.

However, there is now a noticeable multicolor hue in the sky that appears to combine with the precipitation of the land. Showering the people with strangely warm, multicolored liquid. It is all rather much to take in at first. Them being ignorant to the fact that they are in an alien barrier and all.

What would you assume if you were pelted with translucent drops of rainbow liquid every time it rained? Surely you would question the hell out of it. Especially after such a brutal war with forces lacking any sort of humanity.

Such hysterical questioning is exactly what transpires amongst the survivors after the first rainfall. Only for them to eventually come to accept such fates upon experiencing the same strange happenings during every storm. They come to accept the bizarre events so much that as the days pass, people actually become anxious to see exactly what sort of devastation has been wrought to the land outside their commune.

Their curiosity boils up to a point where four groups of four humans venture out on horseback the first week after the war's end to see what they can find. Each one taking off in a different direction in order to properly address all fronts. Ensuring everyone that they will turn around and return after a week's time—no matter what.

After the explorers' departure, the survivors' outlooks are optimistic. However, the first week with no return, the people's optimism begins to wane. Once the second passes the, "Well, maybe's," begin. Now, after the third week goes by, people are a hot mess. Some go stark raving mad waiting for one of the groups to return and tell them the status of the rest of the world. Going as far as becoming violent with others and destroying parts of the settlement over their bewilderment.

All of the more rational people begin settling down and getting into their own groove after that first month. Trying their best to not take any notice of the groups' absence. Those that do primarily stick to daydreaming; keeping the thoughts of what the explorers might find tucked away in the deep recesses of their minds. The more extroverted ones joke amongst their families and friends to cope with their possibly damning plight.

This being because one cannot dwell on the negatives for too long. It will eventually takeover one's mind. Meaning the survivors have to do whatever they can to get their heads on straight and begin working toward a better tomorrow. Else they risk losing it all over their own paranoid delusions.

Just as the newly formed colony begins to settle after the first month post-war, one—and only one—of the explorers makes it back to the settlement. The only thing is, the sole explorer to return comes back appearing emaciated and close to death atop his burned and battered steed. Of which suddenly drops to the ground at the edge of the settlement. Forcing the man to crawl toward the nearest group of humans on his hands and knees while desperately shouting out, "Don't go past South Pass City!"

Shortly after the returning explorer finishes speaking, blood begins pouring from his eyes. He then begins ferociously ripping out chunks of the hair on his head. The hysterical outburst causes the crowd that forms around him to quickly distance themselves. Especially when he begins speaking once more. Choking on each word as he desperately attempts to warn the others, "Don't—go—pass—"

Before he is able to finish his cautionary statement, blood begins spewing from the man's mouth. Its velvety crimson coating his chin, as well as the entire front of his torn and tattered shirt. He manages to throw up his arm to point south (in the direction of South Pass City) before beginning to regurgitate chunks of his innards. All before suddenly descending to the ground and expiring upon contact with his own bloody entrails. Emitting a loud gurgle into the gory mess that sounds as though he is still trying to speak.

However, the man's final muffled words are entirely unnecessary by the end of his dramatic display. All the onlookers needed to know is that he was from the southern search crew. For his demonstration of the outcome if they fail to take his cautionary advice is enough to sway even the boldest of minds from venturing too far.

After word of the horrendous spectacle spreads, people become petrified of leaving the confines of the settlement. The distraught survivors begin talking of radiation poison and nuclear warfare. Others begin questioning their existence and why they were chosen to survive. Most are curious as to whether or not any others have survived the blasts and if the loved ones they left behind might still be out there waiting. No one is really sure and no one dares to answer these meaningful questions. Mainly for fear of the hysteria that they all know will instantly ensue.

As time passes after the incident, the people's paranoia begins to wane. Instead of fear and remorse, the survivors are forced to focus on naught but self-preservation. Once they recollect their sanity, the people begin banding together to build shelters in the forests surrounding Fiddlers Lake.

With most of the survivors having arrived in early August after the initial retreat, they become quite accustomed to the electricity present at the camp grounds. After the war ends in late September, it nearly forces them to quit such luxuries cold turkey. Due to the fact that the carpet bombing done at the end of the war knocks out all of the country's power structures, the people are forced to use the few gas generators they have to continue producing electricity. However, the vehicles soon become unusable after all of the gas and oil is siphoned and drained. Forcing them to begin rationing and eventually discontinuing the use of such unsustainable crutches.

That is not saying the few intelligent and highly-skilled survivors have not already begun to build and forge what they have needed since the moment they got there. They have been working feverishly to get everyone prepared. Utilizing the resources from their cache of vehicles to do so.

Those that have already begun building the new civilization by the war's end are certainly an asset. They are the ones that help the other survivors get their heads out of their asses and look toward the future instead of the past. Their work being what gives them a much-needed shove in that right direction.

Although the more driven individuals have been trying all along to get the people on such paths toward success, the sole explorer's return is what really forces the realities of their plight to finally begin settling into the minds of the majority. Many of whom have seemingly become content with their simplistic environment during the explorers' absence. Only doing what they have had to in order to get by; nothing more, nothing less.

The sole explorer's gory return forces them all to come to the sudden realization that in order for them to be able to survive the fast-approaching winter, the survivors will need shelters with a built-in heat source. A fact that forces the people to band together and build as many primitive shelters as possible in a month's time. Each individual learns new skills as they progress day by day until a new community is born. All from naught but fire, scrap metal, nature, and sheer human will.

Once their new settlement is built, the survivors begin taking ownership of the primitive structures. Encasing them in rocks, grass thatching, and mud as they see fit. Not only to retain the heat, but to add their own little bit of pizzazz to them as well. Making themselves feel all the more at home.

Surely, Fiddlers Lake is the optimum location to start anew. It being a campsite that has been established for a century by this point. Complete with a plethora of natural resources and untamed lands. Still, most of the survivors had never even heard of such a place until weeks before fleeing there.

Being away from the ranges, the artificial environment around Fiddlers Lake stays a consistent seventy degrees for most of the year. But even with the artificial atmosphere being cast from the alien amulet, the winter snow along with its bone-tingling chill still seem to find their way through. Winters there are brutally cold and are always accompanied by heavy snowfall. One definitely has to be sheltered and have a continuous source of heat to sustain.

Without their advanced gadgetry at Fiddlers Lake, civilization becomes primeval. This being due to the fact that a majority of the survivors are accustomed to the help of technology's gentle hand. Seeing as how the greedy banksters forbade many of the manufacturers of yesteryear from making anything that lasts, the survivors are fairly screwed in that department. Planned obsolescence *is* the name of **their** game.

Due to the banksters' monopoly on education, media, and law prior to the war, a great deal of the people in the post-apocalyptic settlement are ignorant of the most basic survival skills; let alone have the knowledge to fabricate electric generators and an elaborate power grid system. Most of the survivors are essentially a step above useless in such departments. Lucky for them, they have that initial step difference between useful and useless. For there are many steps of learning and different directions they can take in order to advance themselves.

With the few distractions currently presented to hinder the survivors' paths, they can each easily master any particular sort of skill in a rather short time period. Of course, the more distractions, the more time it will take to achieve mastery. This being due to the fact that the proper neural networks in the brain must be formed and conditioned over time for such feats to occur. Routine and discipline is what works best in most circumstances.

With them being forced to use what little they have and make the best of it, few of the survivors are fully prepared. But at least they have each other; along with copious amounts of determination and free time. Something that ultimately forces the populace to band together in order to return to their hunter/gatherer roots to survive. Just as it was in prehistoric times, women and children are now the designated gatherers. Men, on the other hand, are the designated hunters.

Overall, people are wary of what they hunt and collect. Radiation poisoning is a very real superstition to them and nothing can be trusted in their frail minds. However, most of the big game fled deep into the ranges during the blasts and have yet to return to their original scavenging grounds. Meaning the people are forced to pick what they can and ration the meat they had brought so they do not prematurely diminish their supply.

Thankfully, berries and herbs are plentiful for the settlers at a special grove full of various fruit trees and shrubs located at the base of Moe Peak. People soon begin calling it the Life Grove. For over time, it becomes their main source of fresh vegetation. Especially since people are far too afraid to wander too far from the settlement.

After a year in isolation, the people start becoming stir-crazy. No one ventures too far from the settlement for fear of radiation death and no other survivors ever come to reveal themselves. Even with the many gardens within the settlement and the plethora of fresh vegetation out in the surrounding woods, people start falling ill from eating rotten foodstuffs and drinking tainted water.

Those that fall ill do not blame such happenstances on ignorance or laziness, but on radiation poisoning. Even though that is not the case, they still manage to poison the minds of many with such contemptable lies. Accelerating their emotionally fraught souls' journey toward despair. Driving them deeper into the dark abyss that their frail minds have now become.

Nearly everyone in the settlement is disconsolate by this time. Most have come to the ungodly revelation that mankind is on its last leg. As well as the fact that they are more than likely going to die in the Wind River Range. An epiphany that is soon followed by the realization that the rest of their species is surely to suffer the same fate shortly thereafter.

With such thoughts brewing in such feeble minds, it is only a matter of time before people begin losing all sense of civility. A feat that does not take long to transpire after their first year. Because once such entropic nightmares start brewing in the backs of their minds, the survivors begin turning to crime to satiate their lust for material possessions. They simply feel as though they deserve everything because they have lost it all.

Those crazed survivors that feel as though they have nothing else to lose risk it all in order to get themselves ahead. A truth that becomes all too real when commonplace thefts evolve into commonplace murders. For the savages soon begin banding together and murdering their victims.

Whether they are conscious or not, it does not matter to one that has nothing to lose. Some even begin turning to cannibalism as their fresh meat supplies begin running bare. Their victims' possessions are merely a bonus for them on their wretched path toward oblivion.

Such unabated chaos boils up to a point where a group of like-minded civilians that want to bring peace band together. They then clash with a notorious clan of cannibals whom have been given the moniker, Adreno-Kuru Cannibals. This being due to their satanic blood rituals. In which they torture their victim for hours before harvesting their adrenaline-laden blood

(Adrenochrome). Only to go on feasting upon their bodies after their death. Committing such vile acts before stealing their belongings and burning down their homes.

It should come as no surprise that the cannibal group's ending has been long overdue. Even after their first atrocity people begin seeking ways to end their despicable crimes. But such a task is easier said than done.

For you see, the clash that brings the clan down is fought primarily with primitive tools, hand-forged knives, and various-sized rocks. Such being because all of the high-tech weapons are sealed off in an armory outside of the settlement and are only accessible to a privileged few. It is one of the few, yet universally accepted laws in the settlement: that the more precise munitions are to be reserved for hunting game—not people. They all have come to understand that those precious commodities have now become rarities and need to be rationed properly.

However, that is not saying that nearly all of the more wise and well-natured civilians do not have caches of self-made swords and guns hidden in their huts. They all do still believe in the American Constitution and its inherent Bill of Rights, mind you. That being because it just so happens to take such beneficent objects to quickly bring the inhuman cannibals to their knees.

The conflict between the inhuman cannibals and the sensible survivors lasts a mere forty-eight hours. For that just so happens to be how long it takes for all of the cannibals to be overpowered and brutally murdered. Just as they had done to all of their prior victims. Ensuring the leaders that have been instructing such heinous acts against their remaining human species members endure the most suffering. As to ensure they each receive their own fitting punishments for the evils their subordinates have been wreaking on their innocent victims.

During the course of the battle, the group of nearly two hundred cannibals are slain. Less than half a dozen of the sensible survivors sustain minor injuries, and a large portion of the settlement is burned to the ground. Upon assessing the damage in the immediate aftermath, those that were not awake get their sudden jostle in the right direction. They quickly come to realize that it can never happen again if they want to survive and prosper through such trying times.

Everyone by this time knows humanity is on its last leg. They know that they must do everything in their power to carry on for their posterity's sake. So once all of the slain are buried in the blood-soaked soil, a group given the moniker, The Order, is formed in the cannibals' innocent victims' memory. The group swears on their good names that they will do whatever they can to help the people rebuild after the skirmish...

Chapter V
The Order

The Order starts out as a small militia with nothing but good intentions. It is formed by a group of three men that are given the simple nickname, the Elders. They are given this moniker due not only to their seniority, but to their infinite wisdom as well. Because they are able to utilize their extensive knowledge and skills to bring peace and order back to the settlement. Something they effectively and quite easily do with the aid of America's Constitution and the structures found therein.

Once they take the reins, the Elders usher in an era of peace and prosperity amongst the small community of survivors that is unparalleled throughout all of human history. To kick-start such miraculous endeavors, the Elders recruit a band of good-hearted survivors that want to protect the people from violence and crime. They then direct their band of do-gooders to aid the other survivors and help them thrive. A feat they accomplish by simply bringing everyone together and giving them various opportunities to build knowledge and trust.

After the Elders bring their community together, the darkened ambience hovering over the survivors finally begins to dissipate. Instead of the constant fear and panic residing in everyone's minds, there is now naught but hope and joy. Because shortly after coming together and setting aside their minor differences, everyone begins peacefully coexisting. People help each other survive and thrive once more. But this is due mainly to the fact that the Elders quickly take care of any sort of threat that presents itself within the settlement. In a peaceful, negotiable, and nonviolent way, mind you.

The Elders also gather everyone together to educate them on the proper techniques of building actual log cabin homes; not the archaic huts with mud insulation and thatched roofing they have become accustomed to. With those simple, yet arduous directions, the survivors effectively mold their settlement into a more comfortable, city-like environment. One that allows humanity to evolve and prosper once more.

With the philia, or in Aristotle's words, "the flesh and blood fraternity amongst the citizens", present in such circumstances, the surviving White humans are more than capable of anything they put their minds to. Them having already demonstrated such feats before the disaster and all. Speaking of which, one must take into account that ignorant tyrants were the ones behind said disaster. Them having set humanity up for failure through their millennia-long Malentian schemes and all.

Having a keen knowledge on such integral topics as species homogeneity within stable civilizations, the Malentians programmed the tyrants to intentionally integrate alien subspecies throughout all of the lands on Earth in order to destabilize them with ethnic strife. They then set up various religions and class systems in order to create further strife amongst the already divided masses. To top it all off, they proceeded to start endless wars and create countless alphabet agencies within the governments to act as money drains. In order to tax the living hell out of all of the citizens.

Such despicable beings got filthy rich through their complex taxation and deceptive billing schemes alongside the usury tacked atop their loans. All the while providing little to nothing of use or value to humanity. Other than borrowing *their* currencies, the tyrant cabal of yesteryear did naught but leech off the many through the thieving *services* they themselves set up. Thus, demonstrating the depths of human depravity. Of which evidently has no bounds.

With that being said, The Order is surely not without its faults. For evil is always residing in the deepest depths of a corrupt human's mind. In the case of The Order, the governance simply grows too quickly for its own good. As the years pass, people begin confiding in their leaders for everything and place their full faith in them. As it has been with any position of power in human history, a select few members that have become overtaken by the Malentians' corruption seek to attain the Elders' position. In order to end humanity once and for all.

But before they are able to act against the Elders, the corrupt Order members get their wish. Because just a few years after founding The Order, when things could not possibly get any better within its now tight-knit community, the Elders pack up their equipment on the eve of the Autumnal Equinox and take off into the night. An event they will soon come to regret.

Fear is big business, or so they say. The more fear and scare tactics, the better. It *is* all about control. Is it not? One would assume the more fear instilled would equate to more control. Making the constants fear and control dependent upon one another. Therefore, a person or a group of people with the power to create fear, to create mass hysteria, now they should be marked as the controllers. Such controllers are precisely what The Order evolves into in order to reign in the populace after the Elders' disappearance.

Upon the sudden disappearance of its founders, The Order quickly begins devolving into a malicious entity. The corrupt waste no time becoming a major threat to everyone in the settlement with their sick sadistic minds. Such minds beginning their atrocious behavior with the punishing of criminals, who are now given radical punishments related to their crimes.

The Order's punishments are thus that thieves' hands are severed, rapists are castrated, and murderers are killed in the same fashion in which they had killed. Essentially every action has an equal, yet opposite reaction. Mainly in order to make examples of the perpetrators. As to deter others from committing the same sinister acts.

By them issuing such violent penalties, no one in their right mind dares to defy The Order. With their attained clout, it is only a matter of time before things inevitably spiral out of control. Ensuring the Malentians' plans come full-circle once more. Circling straight back to humanity's complete annihilation.

With such large amounts of pseudo-fear residing in the minds of the common folk, The Order's seeds of power are effectively sown. As their power matures, it evolves. Mimicking that of the Malentians' protocols. Branching off from severe punishments to smear campaigns against nonsensical rubbish in order to form new laws. This, in turn, leads to the formation of the Breed Laws. But we will get to that later.

You need to understand something that becomes clear the moment laws start flowing freely in the new society: it is the beginning of the end of peace amongst mankind. Peace is simply unattainable by any means. At least not when the Malentians' corruption is present in the minds of men.

You see, peace and freedom just does not seem to balance out when slightly evolved humans ascertain massive amounts of power over an irregular assortment of other humans. There are highly evolved, average evolved, and less evolved human species in society. When the less evolved and average evolved greatly outweigh the highly evolved in a civilization, you get a gullible populace. With said populace, it is easy to take control and bring *order* in times of *chaos*. Or so they want you to believe.

It only takes a single group of hell-bent tyrants with a lust for power and the ability to instill fear in the minds of men to take control of a civilization. With them having the ability to manipulate fear and conquer the populace's emotions, the tyrants have absolute power. When handling such power, one cannot be held accountable for their actions. It will inevitably lead to their hasty demise. Meaning they must have control of any and all beings in society to properly reign over it. Whether it be through blackmail or death is up to their subordinates.

Even if they are unable to outright dominate the people through extortion and arbitrary killings, the corrupt have many other avenues of deception they can utilize to get what they need. Such as bucking the negative hype directed at them with more fear mongering to distract the populace from their diabolical schemes. Or perhaps they could utilize the tried-and-true tactic of accusing the naysayer individuals of committing one of the many atrocities they are trying to cover up. Effectively getting the majority to turn against the corrupts' rivals and, if they are lucky, killing them too. Forever lying to the public in order to perpetuate an infinite loop of shit that forever plays out in their favor.

Well, you know what people say; "Shit rolls downhill." A fact that becomes apparent once the almighty leaders begin utilizing fear tactics to reign over their mindless human cattle. Representing them with their own personal beliefs void of any scientific logic or fact. Forcing all of humanity to suffer for their own selfish gain. Just as it was before the disaster.

With the corrupts' insatiable thirst for power on full display, the people quickly come to realize that such a thirst can never be quenched. These facts become all the more exacerbated when the corrupt minority begins surrounding themselves with loyal brainwashed drones that do anything they command. Forever strengthening their hold over society. Because with their loyal following, the minority rule is able to extinguish any sort of unrest before it ever has a chance to spread. Allowing them to dwindle down societal beliefs and freedoms until there is naught but unintelligible scraps left for their now enslaved populace.

To sum it up simply: absolute power corrupts absolutely. One must never forget that. For that is precisely how the Malentians want things to be. They want chaos and corruption. Sustained entropy is their game. Something that becomes quite apparent after the disappearance of the Elders.

Basically, the absence of their three wise and devout founding Elders has devastating consequences on the survivors. Because shortly after their sudden disappearance, three new sit-in leaders appoint themselves to the highest ranking in the settlement. Only for them to go on calling themselves the Top Three. A fitting name for a trio of self-obsessed tyrants.

Now these three narcissistic men are not as wise or as kind as their predecessors. Quite the opposite, actually. For they turn out to be more ignorant and brutal than Proditor himself. Making it seem as though they took a few chapters out of his book. Except now they are running free with it. Elaborating on their late President's evil plans. In order to further codify the Malentians' fatal system and bring about their competition's demise.

Even with their new leaders' stringent rule, the people slowly begin transitioning into a more relaxed and worry-free lifestyle. The complete absence of criminal activity alone is reason enough for one to not worry. However, as the people begin growing more comfortable with The Order's new brazen leadership, the Malentians' seeds start growing evermore larger.

These foul seeds grow ever so slowly over the years in the minds of the enslaved. For one cannot rush complete control. It is a long and delicate procedure, you see. Something the Malentians have discovered in their extensive past dealing with humanity.

The Top Three play right into such diabolical schemes. Following right along on their predestined route to oblivion. Doing so slowly over the first couple of months as to not alarm the people. Because if such schemes are rushed and the citizens are not thoroughly depressed and downtrodden without an ounce of fight left in them, their satanic schemes will surely fail.

To abate such outcomes, the Top Three allow the populace to do as they please during their first few weeks as leaders. Punishing only the criminals to ease the people's minds. As time passes, the Top Three become preachers. Chanting their self-minded beliefs to the people. Forcing them to follow their word—or else. They do this at first with mere threats. In order to get the rest of the naysayers onboard, those threats inevitably evolve into naught but atrocities involving violence. But such is when their seeds of control finally reach maturity.

Said seeds come to fruition several months after the Elders' absence. Doing so upon the first public beating of a group of rebels by the, now, large group of Ordermen; as members of the Top Three's standing army soon come to be known. You see, there comes to be vast numbers of men who want to join The Order's ever-growing military complex. Men with a thirst for power, as well as patriots who just want to protect their families and friends, grow amongst their ranks.

With such devotion being demonstrated amongst a majority of the brainwashed citizens, it soon becomes mandatory for a man to join The Order's army. An act which effectively unites those that are easily influenced by the Malentians' evil. Joining them together to form a group of power hungry, blood-thirsty tyrants; just like the nefarious Top Three.

Once their army's numbers drastically spike up with the Top Three's ratification of forced-participation laws, the Malentians' corruption soon begins seething inside those with such newfound power. After the evil begins flourishing amongst the Ordermen, all it takes is a single whisper of mutiny and one is a goner. Even speaking the word in rumor or other sorted banter means certain death. Because anyone who speaks of such dissent is publicly beaten—sometimes to death.

Such beatings become a harsh reality for the innocent to swallow. They effectively cause even more fear and panic to begin spreading throughout the settlement. But you see, it is not only being spread amongst the citizens. For the Ordermen themselves especially have to watch their tongue.

Yes, the loyalist Ordermen must watch what they say and do as well. Because during truly corrupt times, a person has to always look out for number one. That is just the way it goes. No one can ever truly be trusted. Especially without the ability to properly distinguish the corrupt from the pure in the midst of such a wicked and faulty system. One in which just simply stepping out of line could mean certain death.

Overall, the Top Three turn their settlement into a horror show. They make their environment as tumultuous as possible. Trying their best to mimic exactly how society was before the war. Just as the Malentians' protocols embedded in their DNA dictate. Keeping the entropy sustained *is* their main priority. Because we are not allowed to live in this Universe in a state of peace. At least not with the Malentians present.

Seeing as how a state of disorder is bound to reach equilibrium if it is left alone, the Top Three's goal is to keep things as chaotic as possible until the great finality. One in which everything dies. There is no escaping such fates. Unless, of course, your species is granted access to use one of the Judex Sapiens' and Sagacians' fabled spheres.

Said spheres have taken the alien species googolplexes to complete. Just like the JUDEX SPHERA in the Malentians' possession. Except they use theirs for all the wrong reasons. Perpetrating their evil on all of the developing species in the Universe. Focusing mainly on the Homo sapiens on planet Earth.

For they are their most evolved and versatile puppets thus far. Meaning their programmed seeds of destruction are easily able to spread and mature with each passing day.

To aid in the growing of chaos in the settlement, laws become commonplace amongst the three devious leaders. They basically ditch the founding Constitution the Elders had taken from America's initial Constitutional Republic and instead form their society into a full-blown oligarchy. One rife with tyranny. Whose leaders form laws against anything and everything they deem inappropriate. All while forgiving those committing the cruelest atrocities; as long as they are in their favor.

The trio essentially create enough laws and loopholes to make the innocent guilty and the guilty innocent. Just as it was under Proditor's Administration, they utilize their ever-growing standing army to enforce their obscene laws; with violence if necessary. Allowing them to form laws out of thin air in order to force the populace to bend to their will. Such as the aforementioned Breed Laws.

You see, the Breed Laws are now the main laws of the land. They are such that any child under the age of sixteen is now a dedicated gatherer. Girls over the age of sixteen are deemed as the reproducers to maintain the status quo. Boys over the age of sixteen are forced into the army. Where they learn how to hunt for food and survive on their own. As well as how to patrol the settlement and harass the people properly.

Those who oppose these laws are exiled out of the settlement. If they demonstrate any sort of physical resistance, they are slain on the spot. There are exceptions, however. Such as if someone is too weak to be of any value to The Order. In laymen's terms: the sick and the elderly. Those "worthless eaters" who fit into said categories are cast out to the outskirts of Fiddlers Lake to live with others who have been deemed non-contributors. Living in an area that soon comes to be known as Death Valley.

Death Valley is located off of Lower Silas Lake roughly two miles southwest of Fiddlers Lake. Most of the children that are forced out to Death Valley are malnourished. Mainly because all of the older villagers living in the valley are simply unable to hunt. They instead rely on their ability to forage, identify, and prepare edible plants. This being due primarily to the fact that they have no advanced tools to hunt with or livestock to either ride or breed for food; only what nature randomly provides.

The emaciated folks do get food scraps brought from Fiddlers Lake. But most do not consider it nourishment. You see, members of The Order *will* bring the Death Valley citizens food after their bountiful feasts. But they seldom make enough extra to feed the ever-growing population there. They also rarely ever make it there in a decent time after finishing their feasts.

One must take into consideration the fact that during most of the year, time is essential for perishable foodstuffs. If the Ordermen leave the food in the scorching heat too long (something they always tend to do), the food spoils before it is delivered. Seeing as how Death Valley is the last thing on the Ordermen's list, the food rarely reaches its final destination.

Instead, the remaining food scraps at the settlement are fed to the livestock. You know, the things The Order actually has a use for. Something that causes the animals at Fiddlers Lake to grow fatter. All while lessening the chances for the children in Death Valley to ever become hunters—or live beyond the age of sixteen. For they either make it through the mandatory conditioning course, or die trying.

That is right, in order to become a hunter in The Order and join the army's ranks, one has to go through a rigorous physical and mental conditioning test administered by the Top Three. No male in either of the settlements is exempt. It is an exam which just so happens to take place on one's sixteenth birthday. No matter what date that may be.

When else is a better time to have your life turned around and flipped upside down than on your sweet sixteen? A male's life is most certainly shaken to its core during such endeavors. Because the conditioning test truly is an upending and traumatizing ordeal. One that starts off in the beginning as a brutal obstacle course. Only to evolve into a fifteen-day ordeal with no salvation in sight. All of which begins at the water hole a half mile southeast of Fiddlers Lake.

This is no ordinary water hole. It is one that has come to be known as Rán Lake. Due to the fact that the bodies of those lost in the water never seem to turn up. Making it seem as though the goddess truly does ensnare her victims' bodies with hempen binds before dragging them down into her depths. Doing naught but rotting away in her lonely abyss; never to be seen again.

Even from the start of it, the course is extreme. Because from the get-go, one has to endure a half-mile sprint from Fiddlers Lake to Rán Lake. Doing so while dodging scores of various-sized rocks that are being randomly catapulted up in the air from behind them.

Seeing as how the rocks travel on a parabolic path from their archaic death machines, they are able to gather enough momentum to do some serious damage if they make contact. Just one hit could take a person out for good. Ending their short and miserable life with a crushing blow to the head. Of which would be preferable to the instant ticket to Death Valley otherwise. No matter one's injury.

That is not even the worst of it. If they make it past the rock sprint, the participant must dive into the water hole and retrieve one of the many broadswords that have been thrown randomly into its depths. If one is lucky, they will be able to find one close to shore. But rarely, if ever, is that the case. Even when they do, the participant must continue swimming over to the other side. One that is nearly a thousand feet away, mind you.

Just imagine doing the course in the winter. Even a trained body would find it excruciatingly difficult to make it through. The human body's cold shock response *is* the leading cause of death in most instances. Even those that voluntarily break through the ice to retrieve a blade are at risk. For if they do not perish from the initial trauma, they still have less than thirty minutes in the lake's icy waters before their body succumbs to hypothermia's deleterious effects. Less than ten if they cannot easily escape.

Now, the lake is a task in itself. After it, the participant has to transition straight out of the water into a rusty barbwire field to get back on land. A field of tetanus that is stretched merely three feet above the ground. Continuing on for roughly fifty feet. Coming complete with sagging spots of wire from those in the past that were struck by its rusty thorns.

After the fifty-foot stretch of hell, the course leads the participant to a rope wall. Before which they are only given another three feet to work with. Meaning they have to pull themselves up out of the barbwire with the rope while contorting their bodies to avoid the certain misery that will soon follow otherwise. That is unless they *want* lockjaw.

Basically, one would have to have a death wish to bestow such a fate upon themselves. Because once over the rope wall, the course leads the participant straight out into the wilderness. Leaving them with naught but their damp, muddy clothes and a rusty broadsword in a decrepit scabbard tied around their waist.

However, the course's participants are not alone. Instead, they are watched over by a horde of Ordermen. All of whom are hiding out in random trees along the rest of the course. This being due to the fact that after the course is completed, one must head down south to Cow Lake and live there the remaining fifteen days of their test.

If the participant veers off from their designated half-mile roped-off route down south to Cow Lake, they are killed for treason. Therefore, such digressions happen rarely, if ever. At least not after witnessing the first defector's horrifying fate. Him having been tortured to the point of crippling before being tossed into Rán Lake.

The poor lad drowning to death after enduring such an extreme punishment surely strikes fear into all other future participants. Primarily due to the fact that they are forced to hear the story over and over again from their parents. Forever cautioning them beforehand to just simply stick to the path.

What sucks the most is that no matter the time of year, the adolescents are tested on their sixteenth birthday. Which means that in the wintertime it is essential to have your birthday close to several others. That way the fires at Cow Lake never have a chance to burn out. Making the fifteen-day excursion all the more enjoyable.

That is right, some of the Ordermen get to spend their time at Cow Lake with others that have similar birthdays. Even sharing the course if they are lucky enough to have been born the same day. With the multitude of children being born during this time of repopulation, it is nearly guaranteed that many adolescents are going to be there during one's fifteen-day period. A time in which they must build bonds of trust and accountability amongst themselves. It is either group up or perish alone.

Now that is not saying that some of the participants have not resorted to cannibalism to satiate their hunger pains. Although it is unknown as to why one would resort to such revelry knowing full-well they will not be alive much longer afterward. Especially when the Top Three hear about their transgressions.

Once again, such events rarely ever happen. When they do though, it is far from pleasant. One would have to be lucky to survive the beating that ensues after such vile acts. Even if they do, they are cast out to live the rest of their crippled life in a torturous hell. Only to die shortly after from dehydration.

It is needless to say, Darwinism thrives in these times. Because it is all about the survival of the fittest. Especially in the Top Three's eyes. So much so that one's physical apex must be obtained prior to even attempting their brutalizing course. If not, death will surely be a constant threat working against them. Forever lurking in the shadows. Patiently waiting for the opportunity to take their young souls away.

One who is strong with their body but not their mind is far more an asset than one who is the opposite during such a trying course. Due primarily to the fact that every Orderman tested must be able to show that they can physically perform under any sort of duress. Something they will certainly have to demonstrate out in the wilderness with the other hunt groups.

That is not saying that such a punishing event does not require immense mental fortitude as well. Because if one is weak-minded or if they simply lack morals and any sort of basic decency, they are quickly put in line by the others. Meaning they get their asses kicked to straighten them out. For such brutish force is necessary when relying on others to survive. It is either you are a part of the team, or you are cast out to the other side of Cow Lake to fend for yourself.

Those that are cast out from the group more often than not become fodder for the surrounding wildlife. If they do manage to survive, the loners are cast out to Death Valley. Where they have to spend the rest of their lives fending for themselves with nothing but the natural resources provided by the planet. So essentially, failure is not an option in most cases.

Regardless of their societal status, those that fail The Order's conditioning test are cast out to Death Valley and are forever branded as failures. It is simply a lose-lose situation. One that boils down to the fact that the Top Three would rather see the young men die than see them bring dishonor to their ranks.

The hunters' children growing up around Fiddlers Lake have a great advantage over the children raised at Death Valley. For you see, the hunters at the lake begin training their children at a young age. Children being raised at Death Valley really have no one to turn to but themselves. Not to mention the hunters and their children at Fiddlers Lake get to feast on the main meals; not just foraged plants and rotten scraps.

Unless the people at Death Valley are educated enough to identify and properly prepare edible plants and trap small game, they are more than likely going to either end up starving to death or become prey to another scavenging predator. Because very rarely do the Ordermen find the time to deliver whatever scraps they have left after their bountiful feasts. Meaning it is a constant kill or be killed situation at Death Valley. If one is not able to produce something out of nothing, they are left with just nothing. It is a very basic concept.

Because of the fact that most of the men with age living at Fiddlers Lake have prior military training, they are able to help the children around them prepare for their inevitable futures as Ordermen. Demonstrating for them the life-saving skills and abilities they will need while fending for themselves in the wilderness. Essentially guaranteeing their success when attempting the brutal conditioning course.

Those in Death Valley must either learn for themselves or die trying. Unless they can forage and thrive out in the wilderness alone naturally, the young will never make it. For their guardians are barely able to fend for themselves, let alone an entire village of those in the same sad decrepit state. Quite frankly, there is absolutely nothing positive about the situation in Death Valley.

Although, Fiddlers Lake is the complete opposite. If one is able to pass the conditioning test and become an Orderman, their lives are forever changed for the better. Such being a fact that begins to show on the first day. Because once they are able to prove themselves at Cow Lake, the Ordermen are outfitted with apparel fashioned by the Top Three themselves. Each set coming complete with unique embroidered symbols to help others distinguish between all of the different hunt groups.

Due to the primitive cloth dying methods they use to distinguish between both age and rank, the older one gets, the darker their tunic will inevitably become. While all of the young hunters are in whites, bright yellows, and varying orange hues, the older ones are in greens, browns, and blacks. Such being dependent upon how many decades one has served. For they are only promoted to a new color once every ten years.

They are not just plain tunics either. The front and back of the tunics are embroidered with the symbol of their group. A symbol that is designed and sewn exclusively by the Top Three themselves. Even though they utilize their wives' skills and their antique foot-pedal embroidery machines to complete such tasks, they are easily able to fool the people and take all of the credit. Making such a ceremony all the more meaningful for the brainwashed saps.

On the back is a square symbol that covers the entirety of the tunic. The front symbol is circular and encompasses the entire chest area; as to add an extra layer of protection atop the breastbone. Doing what little it can to prevent the breastbone from cracking or, at the very least, cardiac arrest if a member is ever struck in the chest by a raging beast.

Now, after the tunic is dyed throughout the years, one would think the symbols would change with it. However, the Top Three's wives design each embroidery so that they are comprised entirely of inorganic materials; ones that are impervious to dyes. Allowing each symbol to really shine. No matter how many times it has been dyed.

Seeing as how they all must make what they have last for as long as possible, the embroidered route was certainly the way to go for The Order. That way, the embroideries can simply be cut out and transferred from one tunic to another over time. Allowing them to last the duration of each member's lifetime.

This feat of longevity is accomplished by everyone learning the basic skills necessary for survival at the formation of The Order under the Elders' guidance. Skills such as sewing. Not just the sewing of cloth, either. But the stitching of flesh as well. For one most assuredly never knows when those skills will be necessary. They just know it could mean life or death if such a situation ever arises.

It is not only natural to pass those basic life skills on to the youth, but essential in order to secure one's posterity. However, the Malentians have no such plans of self-preservation in mind. Remember, their goal is humanity's utter annihilation from the Universe. Something their current meat puppets, the Top Three, are well on their way to achieving. Complete with their own horde of ignorant puppet savages.

Speaking of whom, once they are outfitted with their tunics, the new Ordermen recruits are given white felt cowboy hats with a smaller embroidered symbol on the front. Along with metal 'O's fashioned out of curved nails woven into both sides of its crown. They are even given wool-insulated slacks and thick, thigh-high cowhide leather boots with tire rubber soles. Seeing as how it is up to the individual Orderman to tailor and insulate their boots with whatever they can to keep their feet warm, most men acquire boots a couple sizes larger to fit more insulation.

Whenever their garments become too worn down, they are simply issued new ones. That being because uniform conformity is what they are after. Meaning all the Orderman has to worry about is tailoring his apparel to fit his own body. As well as transferring the symbol from the old cloth to the new.

Said apparel is crafted into various sizes years in advance and stored in a warehouse with the armaments. All of the outfits are stitched by those who are hand-picked by the Top Three's wives themselves. As in those the trio deem most fit to complete such tasks in a meticulous and efficient manner. That being because the apparel is required to look identical. It is also only to be replenished or modified when directed by the Top Three.

Aside from the apparel, every member is issued a freshly-forged pattern welded broadsword fabricated from scrap car parts. Them forging with numerous layers of different metal elements gives each blade its own unique pattern. With the handles being crafted from the remnants of the decrepit blade the youths retrieved in the course, each sword displays its own slice of individuality.

Due to the vehicle scrapyard they created shortly after their arrival, the survivors have everything a blacksmith will ever need. They utilize such commodities to forge the tools needed to assure their settlement's longevity. But even though the Ordermen's swords are crafted to be used for hunting purposes, they use them to taunt fearful villagers as they arrogantly walk past them. Doing so whilst parading around the settlement and threateningly waving them in the air. Such being one of the—many—perks of becoming an Orderman.

The Ordermen are essentially trained to be menaces to society. They ransack people's houses for necessities; sleep in their beds; and even beat people to death. Entirely going against the founding Constitution and its inherent Bill of Rights the Elders put in place.

Now, the Ordermen are the law. Law, of course, has no consequences for its actions when enforced by the majority. If anyone struggles or fights back with the law, they mysteriously vanish into the night. Never to be seen again.

Any villager who questions the objector's absence is told that the deviant left of their own free will. They are then threatened with death if they make any more inquiries into their absence. Possibly even beaten if they ask an Orderman that is in a foul mood.

Speaking of leaving, one of the worst punishments is when an Orderman catches a person trying to defect. Because upon their discovery, the lucky Orderman immediately subdues the dissident by any means possible before relaying the message to the other Ordermen. Doing so by screaming at the top of his lungs while dragging the nonconformist scum by their hair toward the main fire in the center of the village.

Upon hearing the call, all of the Ordermen rush to be the first one to the flames. Due to the fact that they will (more often than not) be in the presence of the Top Three. Their presence simply dependent on how far the dissenter manages to flee. As well as how fast the Top Three can make it to the flames. Causing Ordermen to fight over the opportunity to show off their brutality in front of their leaders; sometimes even to death.

Terrified of messing up in front of their rulers, the Orderman most ardent to get the spot patiently waits for his victim. Muttering not even a breath as he stands before the almighty Top Three. His heart racing as the sweat dripping down from his forehead mixes with the blood seeping from the fresh wounds on his battered face.

Blood on a victor, whether it be his or not, is viewed in a similar manner as a trophy or badge. They are simply markings to show off one's dedication to the cause. Displayed directly in front of those the saps have deemed to be their *masters*.

A fact that shows when the cortisol now flooding their system causes the devoted Orderman to shake with worried anticipation. Worry due to them being unsure as to whether or not their demonstration of violence will live up to those of the past; as to ensure the Top Three's continued presence at future showings. A failure of which would most certainly lead to their own untimely demise.

With the intensity of the defector's screams growing ever nearer, the Orderman at the fire proceeds to walk toward the flame. Brandishing the provided protective leather gloves hanging on a hooked pole alongside a cache of various-sized fire irons before dramatically putting them on and digging through the irons. All of which are stationed inside of a large metal barrel several feet away from the fierce blaze.

Most victorious souls have the propensity to grab the thickest and most damaging fire iron out of the barrel. They then show off their iron of choice to the Top Three by slashing the air around them. Giving their best possible performance in front their liege lords. Not only to show off their combat techniques, but to gloat in front of their fellow jealous Ordermen as well. Such celebratory events are followed by the Orderman transitioning the iron from swinging through the air to resting in the flames. An act that is accomplished seamlessly with their final fluent swing.

When the first Orderman arrives with the rebel victim, he ties the victim to a large wooden pole that stands mere feet away from the smoldering flames. The second Orderman then takes the cherry-red rod and slowly presses it onto the rebel's flesh. An act which forces most of their victims to let out a blood curdling scream. If they do not scream, the Ordermen make sure they do. A feat they accomplish by taking turns beating the rebel. One with the smoldering rod, the other with the blunt edge of their sword.

Sometimes the Ordermen only strike once. Sometimes twice. Sometimes they beat and slice their victims to death with their weapons. One is never really sure. For it is simply dependent on the monsters administering the punishment at the time.

That is not saying that that is the extent the mindless beasts take it to, either. Because once the punishment is through, the Ordermen gather around their victim. If the victim is still alive, the savages laugh and mock their cries of pain. Doing so before spitting in their victim's face and kicking dirt into their fresh wounds.

Both Ordermen doing so with pure joy over the fact that they are able to administer the rebel's punishment in front of the Top Three. Essentially getting their fifteen minutes of fame in front of their Commanders in Chief. A fact that ultimately leads to most of the victims being executed in show shortly thereafter.

With such brutality reigning supreme it is no wonder that, once again, the survivors' lives are comprised of naught but fear and loathing. But still, they gullibly trust their deceitful leaders. It is not so much trust. It is more so the fact that their conniving leaders constantly preach that there is nowhere else for them to go. The citizens foolishly accept this as fact. So, their *superiors'* reign of terror persists.

Many people seriously think that there is nowhere else but Fiddlers Lake to inhabit. But a few of the settlers know the truth. Said few being their saviors: the Elders. Because miles away there is a secret lair buried deep within the mountain ranges. A lair designed for human survival and longevity. Designed and built by the Elders themselves mere decades ago.

If you do so recall, upon the formation of The Order, the settlement was never comprised of fear and loathing. That was mainly due to the Elders. They are evil's check-valve. The ones that are supposed to prevent such atrocities from occurring. They are the pure, sagacious beings that keep the Malentians and their puppets subdued. Only when they mysteriously vanish without prior notice is when things take a turn for the worse. For without the Elders around to guide the uncorrupt survivors, they are bound to suffer at the hands of the ever-growing corrupt minority.

Just who are the Elders, you may be asking? Well, the Elders are more than just the three Founding Fathers of The Order. That is for sure. You see, the Elders had worked for the US Military prior to the uprising and had amassed quite the following during their employ. Them having to be cooped up together in a top-secret government lab for countless hours every day allowed them to build a great respect amongst one another. One which eventually allowed them to reach a synergy level in which they were able to churn out new genius inventions weekly.

With the help of their 3D printers, the trio was able to design, fabricate, and mass-produce their products by releasing their schematics to the public. Giving others the ability to tinker and toil over them to perfection before releasing their own updated versions to the rest of society; for a usage fee, of course. Thus sharing their successes with the rest of the world. All while improving and perfecting their designs by means of mass collaboration.

Even though they worked in such secrecy, the Elders still came to be world-renowned scientists. They became known by inventing nearly all of the revolutionary technology of the mid twenty-first century. Addressed by the media as; "Doctors 2H, NT, and BR". Denoting their initials in an obscure, yet trendy fashion; as to protect their identities from malicious foreign entities. Meaning no one but those close to them personally ever knew both their names and faces.

Not only were they inventors, the Elders were activists as well. They had begun preaching to the people of the coming end of days on various mediums years before the rebellion. Posting feverishly on internet blogs and buying years of space for printed newspaper columns in advance. Signing off with the same cryptic initials to retain obscurity.

Hell, some people even credit the Elders with starting the rebellion. Even though they simply referenced the words of the Founding Fathers of their country, those words laid strong on ignorant ears. With such truths out in the open for all eyes to read, it soon became apparent what travesties had been wrought on mankind. Those being ones of Malentian descent. As in, the annihilation of all life on planet Earth.

All of the schemes used to topple the great Republics and Empires of yesteryear were utilized once more to topple the American Republic. Open borders; miscegenation; perpetual warfare; unending debt; a foreign-sourced central bank; and the normalization of pedophilia alongside the complete control of all media and education were used for such tasks. Molding the minds of billions to suit their crooked Malentian agenda.

The humans just failed to take into account the rapidly advancing technology of the time. Of which the Elders used to their benefit. Taking advantage of the advanced encryption and security offered with the perfected quantum teleportation method of communication. As well as the advanced blockchain technology developing at the time. Utilizing both simultaneously allowed them to undermine those that would have surely censored their words for going against their mindless tyranny. Instead, they effectively got the information to those desperate enough to seek out the truth for themselves.

It is no wonder why the Elders had a loyal following well before the settlement at Fiddlers Lake. They basically rode the wave of technological advancement from its global inception. Giving them the perfect opportunity to quite literally save humanity from its self-made extinction.

Luckily, many of the Elders' devout followers willfully gave into their incessant preaching and heeded their call to flee to the Wind River Range. Those that did not listen and believed them to be crack-pot doomsayers—well, you already know of their gruesifying fate. The survivors that followed truly begin to believe that they are able to see into the future. For the Elders always seem to be able to predict happenings well before they occur. *Every* prediction they have ever forecast comes to fruition. Before long, they are the most powerful, yet gentle leaders of the new free world.

During their time as leaders, the Elders' power and influence—along with their wisdom—causes other members of The Order to envy them. Those envious few sought to end their reign one way or another. Them being the corrupt Top Three, of course. All of whom simply wanted the Elders' influence over the people to commit their own deviant atrocities against them. However, they knew well in advance about the malevolent trio's plan to dethrone them. So before that could ever happen, the Elders disappeared into the night.

Now there is something you must understand before we continue. A pertinent piece of information must be addressed. Before the war, the Elders led a government-funded project to design and construct a state-of-the-art emergency bunker capable of housing thousands of humans. One that would be self-sufficient with unlimited power generation and guaranteed vegetation for an eternity. Basically, somewhere to evacuate several thousand humans before an apocalyptic event.

Soon after beginning the project is when the saviors make their first contact with the Sagacians. The alien species is easily able to earn the men's trust. Going so far as guaranteeing their safety during the coming storm. Even though they speak to them by using aquatic vertebrates as a catalyst and the men know clear well that the coming storm is one that even the most ignorant of people can clearly see coming, the trio cannot help but believe the profoundly surreal display of such indecipherable impossibilities.

Sagacian encounters truly are events one certainly has to see to believe and never tell a soul about. Lest they want to be deemed mentally ill and institutionalized. You know, cast out from society to be forever pacified; their underlying problems never being rectified. It is certainly an outcome none of the men wish to ever have to endure.

In order to evade such outcomes, the Elders kept their mouths shut about their alien encounters. But even in doing so, the trio knew they could not let such knowledge go to waste. Subsequently, with their fresh alien intel in tow, the Elders shared the Sagacians' messages globally via their encrypted media channels. Spreading their words to whoever would give them the time of day.

Even on the battlefield, the Elders spread their message of guaranteed salvation after the war. Utilizing the citizens' Commuter Bands and cellular phones to accomplish such tasks. Although electromagnetic pulses were sporadically set off during the war, and the neutron bombs used by the invading forces took out many of the signal's transmission towers, there was still hope that someone out there got the message and spread it to others.

Just think about what would have happened if the occupied government ever found out about their own bought and paid for scientists' endeavors. Their heads would have most certainly ended up in a basket. Even with that being the case, they did not waver. Such selfless behavior alongside their immense wisdom is what truly grants them their *Elders* title. Well, their selflessness along with their ability to be able to predict the future—an ability only possible due to their Sagacian encounters.

Although that may be the case, the skill of foresight is still viewed as remarkable to the ignorant mind. However, the Sagacians only seem to reveal what knowledge is absolutely necessary to the Elders. They never seem to divulge too deep. Meaning sometimes the trio must adlib extra material to satiate the more curious minds. Such unsightly misconceptions are the reason why the trio gets lost after they escape from Fiddlers Lake.

With the world governments' strict regulation of any sort of fusion or nuclear energy sources before the war, humanity is never able to advance beyond quantum batteries and fossil energy. Therefore, most technology still relies on such wretched resources to operate. Seeing as how the Elders were commanded by the Sagacians to leave all of their advanced technology at the bunker before the war, they became stuck with the same archaic technology the common folk had at their disposal. Such truths combined with the lack of electricity needed to power their antiquated electronic devices creates quite the predicament.

Paper maps are a thing of the past, mind you. They are ancient technology by this point in time. Even though they had knowledge of the upcoming end of the old world, none of the three men sought to print up such outdated technology.

Hindsight is always twenty-twenty, right? Well, yeah. It takes them a lot longer than it should to find their bunker. Because mysterious premonitions may be able to garner them followers, but they apparently cannot help them find their route. Even if they could, Mother Nature is most certainly not on their side.

For months the Elders traverse through treacherous snowfalls on every mountain they peak; blazing fast streams along every waterway they cross; and even when all seems calm, the predator-infested woodlands are there to smite them down. Forcing them to settle down and camp for weeks at a time in some instances. To them, it seems to be one setback after another. No luck is to be had and no direction is ever easily found.

That is until the Elders finally rediscover their hideout. An event that soon dawns on them as miraculous. Because upon their arrival, they have an epiphany of sorts. It is as if the information of their current whereabouts, along with a far simpler way back to the settlement, is simply put into their brain by a foreign source. Allowing each of them to come to the sudden realization that Fiddlers Lake is only twenty miles away from their lair entrance, which is located on the southwestern side of Mount Chauvenet.

You see, the cave holds many secrets. Secrets that the three Elders can only begin to divulge into and fathom the true capacities of. Yet, upon the discovery of their bunker, they do naught but reminisce over the wonders inside of the caverns that lay before them. All while setting up a temporary campsite in the valley outside of the entrance to the cave and resting their weary minds beneath the starlight.

Instead of going inside, the Elders wake the next day only to quickly turn around and hightail it back to the settlement. Why, you ask? Well for the mere fact that they *know* the caverns are not quite ready for them yet. Also, because the Elders know the longer they are away from Fiddlers Lake, the worse things will become for their kinsmen. If the Elders were to go inside now, they know they will easily become caught up in work. For work is a foul mistress indeed. One that allows a person to elude even the direst of fates.

Equipped with the vital information of their lair's whereabouts, the Elders are now prepared to begin their grand scheme. As in initializing the beginning of the New World. You see, their true goal is to begin a perfect population of uncorrupted humans in the caves. Just as it was foretold in one of the Sagacians' premonitions.

To do this, the Elders plan to travel back to Fiddlers Lake and begin scouting for the perfect bunch of people to begin anew. Preferably those they know are not corrupted by the Malentians' evil. But they know that no matter who they choose, everyone will be willing to take the risk and leave their homes at the lake behind without a trace. For the Elders have a basic idea of the happenings that have transpired during their absence. Them each having similar dreams the night prior of the atrocities wrought upon the innocent settlers by the nefarious Top Three.

It does not take long for the Elders to experience the turmoil firsthand, either. Because upon their entry back into the settlement, they are unexpectedly court-marshalled by The Order. Supposedly due to them being gone a whole six months without any sort of contact or prior warning. But the benevolent trio knows their nefarious stand-ins had most certainly marked them for dead; if not physically, then mentally.

Now you must take into consideration the fact that shortly after the Elders' disappearance last Autumnal Equinox, the Top Three are the first to begin asking questions about their absence. After questioning everyone in the settlement and coming up with nil, they begin making the lives of those who refuse to speak a living hell. But that is all just the beginning of their foul endeavors.

You see, the Top Three want to take the Elders out of commission for good. Doing so all by themselves in order to fully take the reins of civilization without hindrance. Once they are gone, they have to make sure the founding leaders are gone forever. That way they know for sure that they can initiate their plan for total control. A feat they accomplish rather quickly and with relative ease, mind you. Simply following the same Malentian protocols utilized by human civilizations of the past. Poverty and ignorance being the two main factors enabling such hierarchical societies. Both of which are sure to be present in times of disarray.

Whenever the Elders suddenly show up months later out of the blue, the Top Three's plans are already well underway. There is nothing—neither hell, nor high water—that is going to stop them. Meaning the Elders might actually get off the hook this time around. That is, if luck bodes in their favor.

Still, the nefarious leaders had put a bounty on the Elders' heads during their absence. If anyone sees the Elders or their corpses, they are to capture them and bring them directly to the Top Three. With the Ordermen constantly patrolling along the perimeter of the settlement on horseback, it guarantees that someone will eventually see *something*. Because **no one** enters or leaves without the Top Three's permission.

Upon the Elders' entry into the outskirts of the settlement on the morning of a brisk Vernal Equinox, the Ordermen do just as they had been ordered. They stop the Elders before they are able to make it near the town. The Ordermen then arrest them by hog-tying each of them; covering them with hemp sacks; beating the hell out of them; and dragging them back to the settlement tied behind their horses. Dragging them all the way to the ritzy cabins where the Top Three's families reside. All of which are located on the outskirts of the settlement. Far away from the rest of civilization. Just for occasions such as this.

But that is only due to the fact that the rich and powerful feel as though they must be segregated. You know, to live in their own narcissistic fantasy land. Far away from the horrifying scenes they themselves have wrought upon their innocent mindless citizens.

The Elders' initial encounter with the Ordermen confirms the Sagacians' dreamworld premonitions and then some. For the conditions, to them, are far worse than anything they could have ever of imagined on their own. None of the Elders can seem to comprehend how things could have gotten so bad, so fast.

Especially after being beaten and dragged for miles; their minds racing as their bodies skim across the damp forest floor.

With each of the Elders unable to move out of the awkward position they had been forcibly tied into, their minds primarily focus on the pain. Because every rock or branch they make contact with while encased in their frigid hempen tombs effectively halts their train of thought. No matter how complex it may be.

Lucky for the Elders though, the Ordermen eventually get them onto the main trails. Ensuring little, if any, contact is made with said obstacles after reaching such points. For the main trails throughout the settlement are to be spotless and remain as such all year round. Each Orderman doing his part to ensure such conditions are kept. Per the Top Three's orders, of course.

When they finally come to rest and the Elders are freed from their filthy hemp sacks before their new oligarchs, the insidious questions start flowing. In response, the Elders desperately try to plea that they had simply gotten lost on a hunting trip. Each one piggy-backing off the last's story. Utilizing their godlike improvisation skills to make it seem real. Making even themselves believe their intricate web of lies by the end of their worried speech.

No matter how well the Elders perform or how much they live inside of their lies, the Top Three know their story is rubbish. It is not even plausible in their evil, twisted minds. They seem to smell a crock of manure emanating forth from the Elders' mouths from the get-go and refuse to hear any more of their debaucheries upon their completion. Especially coming from the men they know for a fact are the wisest in the land.

Them, the fabled *Elders*, getting lost. Yeah, right. Likely story. Especially a day before the Top Three had planned to execute them. Not in a million years could such coincidences have ever occurred. Not even in their narrow mind's eye.

But even though seamlessly blended debaucheries *are* the case in such instances, and not one of the Elders denies such damning claims, the Top Three still somehow manage to show them pity. Doing so by putting the Elders under eternal house arrest; as to quell their citizens' unrest. Officially putting an end to the rumors about them having executed their original leaders once and for all.

Their restrictions are such that none of the Elders are to be allowed outside of the city limits (which are guarded 24/7 by Ordermen) for the rest of their lives. No one is allowed to speak to the Elders. If caught, they are threatened with serious repercussions for both them and their families. Forcing the trio to live in a humiliating state of shame for the rest of their days.

Except after the Elders' return, something the Top Three never could have foreseen happens: the townsfolk actually refuse the new laws. Instead, the citizens beg for the reinstatement of their original leaders. Simply hoping to end the corrupt ways of the new faction right then and there.

However, the Top Three do not tolerate hearing such blasphemy. They do not use violence this time around though. Instead, after their citizens' unruly outburst, the new leaders become relentless in their attacks against the Elders' character. Using their acquired clout to sway the public view of their predecessors during their weekly ramblings in the town square. Doing so by frequently speaking of abandonment and how they sent out a rescue squad to capture the Elders. Only to be met with force and retaliation.

To explain their beaten bodies, the Top Three say the Elders fought back and did not want to be rescued. Going so far as telling people the Elders have formed a new colony without their devout followers miles away. Ensuring them that the new settlement is where all of the people that have gone missing are. All while making it sound as though the Elders kidnapped them.

With such damnable sentiments being implanted into the malleable minds of men across the settlement, the Elders know they have to act fast. They begin talking to the townspeople they trust most. Desperately pleading with them to help them save what is left of humanity. However, even their most trustworthy of fans and followers will not talk to them for fear of the ramifications.

There are a few, however, that risk life and limb for the Elders. They are those who, unbeknownst to The Order, have already formed a top-secret faction against their nefarious rule. A band of young do-gooders that call themselves, "The Stigmatized"…

Chapter VI
The Stigmata

Upon the Elders' return to Fiddlers Lake, the harsh realities that have come to be during their relatively short time away are revealed. Within their six-month absence, the self-appointed Top Three have segregated the commune according to the varying levels of contributors. The more a family contributes, the higher their social ranking amongst The Order. So those who do not contribute much are cast further away from the epicenter of the lake. Making it that much harder to get their much-needed resources.

One must not forget the non-contributors over in Death Valley, either. All of whom receive nearly nothing from the merciless Ordermen. Well, besides beatings and spoiled foodstuffs. In essence, the Top Three have created an assortment of social classes. They have formed a hierarchy that is divided by how hard their citizens work and how much each of them contributes to the community. It only seems fair, right?

But one has to wonder about the pregnant lady with five toddlers already running amuck. How is she supposed to contribute any food or supplies while caring for her young? With her husband having recently died in a hunting accident, she is desperately struggling to stay on The Order's good side. If she fails to do so, her family will surely be handed their death sentence. That being a one-way ticket to Death Valley.

However, no such sympathy is to be had amongst the Ordermen. The misogynistic pricks will cast an entire family out to their deaths and not bat an eye. Especially if the woman does not *perform* for them. You know, to stay on their *good* side. Lecherous animals each and every one they are. Meaning there really is no way out from such hellish conditions but Death Valley—or more simply, just death.

Sadly though, those aforesaid situations are all far too common throughout the settlement. For it is a time of rebirth for the human race. It is just like the birthrate upticks after World War I and II. Just done in a more drastic and controlled manner on a far smaller scale.

Of course, both World Wars were naught but premature acts of extinction orchestrated by the Malentians. Ones in which the eventual extinction of the White human species, Homo sapiens, and all other species of human shortly thereafter would be certain. Feats that are evidently accomplished rather easily with the use of their programmable puppet governments. Examine the downfalls of all of the Republics throughout human history and you will find demonstrations of such truths.

But even though they have failed every time in the past, the Malentians know that as long as their prey is distracted by their controlled paper currencies and faulty belief systems, anything is possible. Simply observe their subjugation of the world economies throughout the twentieth and twenty-first centuries with their usury-laden fiat monies. The debt from which they have used time and time again to completely subdue nations.

Once their central banking system became thoroughly distributed throughout a country, that country's economy, government, education, and media complexes were all at stake within a year's time. They were easily seized and converted into propaganda machines for the Malentians. For example, America's **third** central bank, the Federal Reserve, was put in just a year prior to World War I breaking out in 1914. At the end of which, the flu pandemic of 1918-1920 broke out. Eventually bankrupting the nation with the Great Depression in 1929 and ultimately dragging them into World War II; which began another decade later in 1939.

Cohencidences are commonplace with the nefarious tribe. Ponder upon the Russo-Ukrainian war, which started a century after World War I in 2014. Continuing on into the COVID-19 pandemic of 2020. Genocidal intentions play out like clockwork with the bestial beings. History is replete with examples of how hastily the Malentians' puppets get to work dismantling the civilized world and ushering in the genocide of humanity after establishing their monopolizing institutions of societal decay in a nation.

The Malentians' programmed route to ruin always begins with the devolution of the homogenized individualist Republics into multicultural majority-driven Democracies; whose corrupt representatives overwhelmingly vote in favor of the degeneration of said Republics. Making it lawful to open their borders to alien human subspecies while bending the minds of the masses to obscure the reality of their actions. All while silencing their critics with speech laws before forcing their radical agenda on the populace.

Faggotry and miscegenation runs amuck during such times due to the puppets' arrogance as well. Because once they have deceitfully conquered a nation, they let it be known. It is all just a historic ritual of humiliation for the cowardly bunch.

What better way to completely overcome and ensure the conquering of a nation than to turn their future men into sissies by poisoning their food and water with endocrine disruptors. All of the media is tailored to further sap one's soul away too. In which the puppets demonize men and masculinity while *liberating* their future mothers. Brainwashing them into thinking that being mindless tax cattle during the day and guiltless whores by night is a more favorable choice than marriage and motherhood.

With the prevalence of abortions and birth control, it makes the females more focused on making money and having casual sex. Rather than settling down and raising the next generation of their species. Thus, ensuring their future survival. It is no wonder why procreation is so frowned upon. It is the complete opposite of what the puppets' masters want to occur.

Each time they have tried the extinction route in the past, the Malentians effectively and quite easily duped the more trusting and civilized human species. They simply used their empathy against them to devolve their societies and create the tumultuous environments necessary for the despots that inevitably follow. Their most recent attempt ultimately led humanity to The Great Bio War that nearly ended it all. Only for them to go full circle with the war's survivors and bring about the current situation at Fiddlers Lake.

No matter the case, the humans corrupted by the Malentians' evil always seem to end up lording over the mutated ones that are immune to such fates. Making it seem as though the Sagacians and Judex Sapiens have their hands in the mix as well. They evidently just go the long-term passive route with their human subjects to retain obscurity.

But what are the innocent people to do in the interim? Where are they to go? Well, the people fail to do jack-diddly squat. They do not go anywhere. Their children, however, now they act with as much courage and assiduity as they can muster.

The children are the only ones with enough time and sense to think of anything besides just their basic survival. So, they utilize such blessings to begin forming a coalition against The Order. Children ARE the future, or so they say. A fact that becomes apparent when the kids all join together to *gather fruits* in the far reaches of the forest nearly every day. Except they are not gathering. Unless you want to call building a kick ass cabin in the woods gathering foodstuffs.

Even so, the children are still technically gathering *something* by constructing a cabin. Because they join together to build with the sole intention of gathering like-minded people to one location. As to conduct secret meetings against The Order in the dead of night. Well out of the way from any prying ears.

These youths know for a fact that nowhere is safe to speak in opposition of the Top Three's vile oligarchy within the community. If they are caught, they are all well aware of the fact that their actions will get them killed. Meaning they have to take extreme precautions, lest they be discovered. In order to adhere to that fact, the children implement several safeguards to protect their behinds.

First and foremost, the children start by selecting an area far away from the settlement. They know they will need to find somewhere far outside of the Ordermen's regular patrolling routes. Somewhere like the valley northeast of Cony Mountain.

Its elevated coverage on the southeast facing portions is reason enough to choose such a spot. That coverage combined with the two-and-a-half-mile distance between themselves and Fiddlers Lake will surely provide them with enough protection to suppress their fire's smoke enough to evade detection.

With their biggest problem, location, taken out of the equation, the children begin crafting the tools they need to build a cabin. Having spent their first decade of life before the war, most of the children had the opportunity to be around and learn from the Elders during the first few years of The Order. Those gratuitous opportunities are now benefitting them greatly.

This being because the Elders made it their prerogative to educate the children. They taught them how to forge their own tools and make anything their hearts could ever desire out of scrap metal. As well as educating them on how to use said tools to build complex structures.

During their time with the children, the Elders taught them valuable skills. Not only about the importance of being independent, but being creative as well. Lessons they still cherish to this day. Because due to those lessons, the children are able to create and build anything they put their minds to. Doing so with naught but fire, metal, and pure determination.

To prove to themselves they have what it takes to go it alone without their wise mentors, the children put their minds to the test by jumping head first into the task at hand. Spending days away from their families in order to accomplish their goals. Risking everything they love and have ever worked for just to claim their independence from their vile oppressors.

The knowledge gained from their mentors' teachings clearly shows when the kids hit the ground running. Because they start off working with flames. As in forging all of their supplies with the aid of a brick furnace. One that just so happens to be constructed out of clay bricks crafted from their makeshift stone kiln. Even the mortar holding the bricks together is made with the powdered clay residue from the kiln mixed with water. Making the scrap metal for the tools and the automatic transmission fluid used for the quenching of said tools the only non-natural materials utilized; each of which are stolen from the vehicles in the junkyard.

In such instances, the stealthier and more difficult the task, the greater the reward; as well as the punishment if caught. Meaning if the children do not have the requisite specialty tools and skills required for the retrieval of their precious resources from the junkyard, they are sure to fail. Because if they take too long and get caught, they will surely feel the wrath of the Top Three.

However, such risks must be taken in order to rise above one's oppressors. Else they be driven straight to their demise. It truly is a predicament in which the victim must act hastily and in good faith. Lest they be overcome with the guilt that comes with inaction. Guilt that rises exponentially once others begin getting hurt due to their apathetic ways.

One either has to buck up and approach the situation head on, or risk losing all of their dignity during the descent into acceptance oblivion. A descent that is led by none other than those that have been corrupted by the Malentians. Beings who are merely following in their degenerative forefathers' footsteps. For all of humanity's genes stem back to those first groups of hominins they corrupted at their inception.

Blessed are those humans that are not corrupt. Humanity itself is blessed that so many people immune to the Malentians' evil survived the war. Not to mention ones that are thriving in clear opposition of the corrupts' ways. Yet, such thriving is only possible due to the skills the youth learned from the Elders' teachings. Skills they have been honing as they proceed forth.

With their plot of land established along with their fortress' blueprints and freshly-forged tools in hand, the children begin their extensive project. Starting off by digging out the outline of their cabin before laying down a cinder block foundation and building up the sleeper walls required for their planned suspended timber floor. Only to begin going to town on the trees within their selected area shortly after. Chopping and sawing them as they see fit to produce the joists and planks.

As long as they can manipulate the wood enough to get their floor somewhat square and level, the children are happy.

Because the task is much easier said than done. Something they come to realize after felling and squaring up their first tree. But that is only due to the tree's enormous stature.

Even though *all* of the trees are massive, the first is always the worst. It is usually the same no matter what substance one is working with. A fact that holds true in this instance. For it takes several trees before the kids are able to really get in their groove.

Once the floor is finished, the children begin squaring up logs for the cabin. No matter how haphazardly they are joined, they chink them together. Utilizing a basic chinking material composed of clay, wood ashes, salt, and water to mix. Just as the Elders taught them before their sudden disappearance. As though they knew the children would need such skills in the near future.

It soon becomes apparent that the children absorbed everything the Elders ever taught them. Because soon after they have the outline done for their planned box gable roof, the children begin making it out of the scrap tree limbs cut off all of the felled trees. Squaring up, sawing down, and joining together the largest limbs to form a frame.

That aforementioned frame is then covered by a blanket of branches before being installed atop the structure. The children form the blanket out of the remnants of their felled trees along with other shrubbery found around the structure. Beginning its many intertwining layers from the bottom up in order to create a more efficient water guard. Something necessary if they want their structure to survive out in the harsh elements.

After it is built, the children proceed to cloak the perimeter of their cabin with transplanted knotweeds. An invasive deciduous plant, knotweeds spread themselves throughout the forest while at the same time growing to massive heights. All while retaining themselves in dense thickets; effectively drowning out the diversity of plant life where they are present. Making them the perfect cloaking agent.

Yes, knotweeds are very plentiful around Fiddlers Lake. As they were all across North America before the war. With the aggressive plant growing in nearly every corner of the woods surrounding Fiddlers Lake, the Ordermen will never suspect a thing if they inspect the area. Because it most definitely appears to be naught but another thick knotweed patch to the naked eye.

Even though deep within the patch of weeds rests a diabolical structure that goes against all of the Top Three's new laws, it is just as inconspicuous and easy to brush off as any other. There is quite literally no way a passing eye would be able to distinguish otherwise. So, with their finely crafted and properly hidden cabin in tow, the children begin spreading the word to their most trusted cohorts in order to recruit members.

Soon after they pass the word, the young rebels' faction begins to grow rapidly and their crowd base diversifies. Citizens of all ages begin gathering at the cabin to sit in the meetings and discuss their plans to thwart their evil masters. Before long, the motley crew of citizens accepts the moniker: The Stigmatized. A name that, to them, stands for freedom and fair justice. Just as the Elders had preached and tried to establish before their sudden absence.

Still, one must take into consideration the fact that the founding members of The Stigmatized are mere teenagers. Teens that have been born from the seeds of those viewed as *less than favorable* to The Order. But even with the shadow of doubt and defamation towering over them, the children have all but accepted their fate.

Instead, they create The Stigmatized to alleviate the negativity cast onto them by their leaders. Clearly giving their oppressors the proverbial middle finger and sticking up for what they know is right. Because instead of allowing such evil to perpetuate and grow in their environment, they rebel.

Once their numbers begin to grow, the leaders of the rebel faction begin fashioning 'S' pendants out of forged nails to promote their cause. Doing so in clear opposition to The Order, of course. For the children fashion the pendants just like The Order's 'O' insignias that are attached to every Orderman's cowboy hat.

After they are finished making their first batch of pendants, the leaders begin excitedly handing them out to all of the members. They then begin mass-producing the 'S' pendants for all of their members to hang throughout the settlement. Effectively evolving the mere rebel formation into an organized symbolic union. All while ensuring that word about The Stigmatized begins to spread.

To show their pride over their newly-founded faction, members of The Stigmatized bravely wear their pendants. Mainly by stitching them to the sleeves of their shirt. There are some though that take the more inconspicuous route and utilize the pockets of their pants. Ensuring they are able to easily hide them from the Ordermen when they are near in order to avoid conflict.

Although some choose to take the more cowardly route, there are some Stigmatized members who go as far as fashioning necklaces out of hempen twine and draping them from their neck. Essentially going the extra mile to show their support. All while opening themselves up for a world of pain around the Ordermen.

No one else really knows what the 'S' stands for. So, upon them seeing the nonconformist symbols, the Ordermen mock the secret members and demoralize them by calling them various cursory names. Names such as: 'Sissy-fuck', 'Stupid-fuck', and even 'Scum-fucker'. They then proceed to beat the snot out of them for trying to be different.

The slanderous name-calling is more for the Ordermen's pleasure. Because it makes them feel better about their atrocious behavior one would suppose. As though such trite curses will ever help prevent their eternal damnation for the physical atrocities they commit against their fellow man.

Faced with such brutality for just basically being themselves, it is no wonder the members of The Stigmatized are three shades past ecstatic upon hearing of their blessed Elders' return. They are so grateful that on the night of their return, three of the founding Stigmatized members split up and creep into their cabins. Each one bypassing the guards outside only to be met with hushed rebuff once inside. A response deemed natural after they come to realize the rough shape their founders are in.

Much coaxing is required to get the Elders to leave their humble abodes. To them, trust is now a hard thing to come by. Especially when their presence alone merited being bound and beaten several hours earlier. By men they knew and trusted a mere six months ago. Luckily, the youths have their ducks in a row and are able to lure the Elders outside with their cunning.

Promises of pride; shock and awe; the ability to lead again; as well as immunization from conflict cause each of them to budge in favor of such mutiny. Because the last thing they want is a repeat of earlier.

With those obstacles already having been thought about and taken care of by The Stigmatized's founders, the Elders are all in for smooth sailing after their initial escape. For them to avoid any unsightly occurrences, they leave body decoys comprised of pillows and sheets beneath the Elders' comforters. Making it appear to the guards that they are sound asleep in their beds. Just to bypass them once more through one of the cabin's retractable crown glass windows before rendezvousing with the others.

Through the forest the leading defilers sneak. Their defamed mentors lagging behind as they furtively traverse through the woods in the dead of night. Exploiting every precaution they can in order to avoid all of the patrolling Ordermen; who are sure to leave death in their wake.

Upon safely reaching The Stigmatized's cabin, the Elders are clearly taken aback by the young neophytes' courage and craftsmanship. But they are proud most of all. For their apprentices' finely crafted hideout spans twenty-feet-wide by thirty-feet-long and stands nearly ten feet off the ground. That is without taking into consideration the roof, which adds an extra five feet to the center.

The entire domicile is composed of logs from various trees. Something that is quite evident with the multicolored bark and varying log sizes. Even so, it is truly a marvel that such young, neophytic humans could muster up enough knowledge and dedication to build such a marvelous structure. All in opposition to their nefarious rulers to boot!

Said neophytes even go so far as fully furnishing their cabin as well. Utilizing all of their felled trees' stumps as chairs. Squaring them up and crafting them down into all kinds of various sizes and designs to compensate for the varying ages and heights of all their members. There is also a brick-and-mortar fireplace in the back to keep it warm in the winter months. As well as tables and a podium; each of which are comprised of brick-and-mortar bases with squared wood plank tops.

To top it all off, there is a long whittled-down tree branch in the cabin's entryway. Complete with a large bloodied cloth hanging on it with their 'S' logo sewn in the center. It is truly a symbolic flag. A flag that waves ever so slightly every time someone walks through the makeshift cabin door.

However, as soon as the Elders walk through the door on that fateful night, one could swear the flag was possessed. Because the moment the door swings open, the flag fully unfurls and their sewn 'S' is all the Elders can see as they enter. Forcing the trio to take a step back in astonishment.

Without even having to say a word, the battered Elders are confronted with the opportunity to lead The Stigmatized. Dozens of desperate and impassioned faces stare hopefully at them in the background awaiting their response. Hoping they will guide them now as they have before.

Of course, the benevolent trio agrees to jump on board and guide the rebels in their cause. Only to begin their work right then and there. Working for several weeks in the reclusive veil of night to hash out a foolproof scheme to overcome their corrupt leaders.

In those weeks following the Elders' return, the Top Three begin transitioning into a state of mind where they have constant fits of paranoiac rage. Making it seem as though they know treachery is to be afoot with the *wretched* Elders' return. Then one day, as if out of nowhere, curfews begin being enforced. Such a curfew being one in which anyone caught out after nightfall is given a swift punishment in the town square. As in they are beaten with a scorching fire iron in front of anyone willing to spectate such atrocities.

But even with such harsh punishments being threatened, the devout Stigmatized members will not be led astray. They cannot afford to give up now. Especially with the omniscient trio at the helm of their organization.

The Top Three's paranoia gets to a point in which they hire spies to keep an eye on the Elders' every movement—at *all* times of the day; as to satiate their inherent distrust in their fellow man. Because in the Top Three's corrupt minds, the Elders are everything they despise. They are the embodiment of purity—of godliness. A trait engrained in the corrupts' mind to be evil. Such a trait, in their minds, must be eradicated; lest the Malentians' plans for humanity's annihilation be ruined.

With The Stigmatized growing more each week due to the growing number of people defecting from The Order's rule, it becomes hard trusting new individuals. This is especially so after The Order begins preaching about the evil powers the Elders possess. As well as how people should report any suspicious activities witnessed amongst their peers; whether they be man, woman, or *child*. Making direct eye contact with The Stigmatized's founding group of teenagers as they take turns speaking. As though they already have a hint about the adolescent's vile practices against their laws.

Even though they took all of the precautions in building their structure, the teens have a much harder time building an organization in which they can fully trust all of its members. Because some humans are just downright corrupt. One cannot trust anyone in such times of depravity. For some individuals simply build up trust to throw it away and betray their *allies* in order to better their own standing amongst their oppressors.

With such vile beings in their midst, The Stigmatized's members know they must exercise preemption—and fast. They know full well they will all be goners if their secret is ever exposed. Meaning extra precautions will surely need to be taken in the immediate future to prevent their discovery.

However, unbeknownst to The Stigmatized's members, a devout Orderman has already infiltrated their ranks. One of their more recent recruits: the town drunkard. No one really notices until after the Top Three's preaching though. For that is when the noted member starts becoming irrational and rowdy at The Stigmatized's random weekly meeting.

The drunkard curses at the Elders and what The Stigmatized stands for. He essentially goes mad that night. Just witchy mad. So much so that before he storms out of the hideout, the drunkard hoarsely begins screaming; "Witchery and trickery!" Repeatedly yelling such phrases while knocking down The

Stigmatized's flag and flipping the bird to the entire room of rebels before his dramatic exit.

Mere moments after the drunkard's departure, the Elders pull the members of The Stigmatized together and ask that the irate member be tracked. They fear the worst of fates has befallen their rebel faction. That being: a spy in their midst. Yet, the members do not seem to worry. Mainly because the man is just a drunkard and always seems to pull irate acts out of thin air.

No one expects such a degenerate to be capable of much else than creating a ruckus wherever he travels. Especially whenever he is deeply saturated in a perpetual drug-fueled state. One in which any human would be incoherently babbling about their self-righteous beliefs and passing judgement whenever they see fit. Due primarily to alcohol's toxic effects on one's bodily systems. Giving reason as to why the members would be so unenthused by such acts from a mere drunkard.

The Elders are right to be cautious though. For upon the first day of tracking the drunkard, he is seen talking directly to the Top Three. It turns out that he is actually a distant relative of one of the nefarious leaders. They simply use his shallow and derelict personality to get him into the rebel faction. Because who thinks much of a drunkard?

Well, the members of The Stigmatized surely do now! Especially since their many prying ears listen to the derelict relay information about the hideout's location and the Elders' whereabouts during the night. Causing their worst fears to come to fruition before their eyes.

At The Stigmatized's next meeting, the drunkard spy is released from the rebel faction. He is threatened with death if he speaks another word to the Top Three of the Elders' whereabouts at night. Except such threats fall on deaf ears. Because mere moments after the drunkard's release, a group of Ordermen descends upon their hideout. Something that is surely a first come first serve reward for the bastards. For the first few men to make it inside are the ones that get the pleasure of hogtying the Elders and dragging them through the woods in the dead of night.

You know the loyalist scum most assuredly fought to the death over such rewards. The victors smiling the entire way knowing damn well they will have the honor of beating the Elders in front of the Top Three. A privilege sought after by the most sick and sadistic beings. More specifically, those that have been corrupt since birth. For no such blind devotion to evil can be described in any other way. Such atrocities against one's own species are naught but implanted Malentian fantasies taking the reins of their feeble human minds.

Demonstrations of such evil become prevalent after the Elders are captured. Because the remaining Ordermen proceed to chase down the rebels and beat them into submission before binding their hands behind their backs with hempen rope. They then proceed to tie them together before walking them behind their leaders to the town square. Periodically stabbing them in the back with the pointed end of their sword's sheath to hasten their gait. As well as to satiate their inherent need to inflict pain on others.

If that is not joyous enough for the sadistic bunch, the last few remaining Ordermen get the opportunity to light the cabin up in flames before departing. Laying waste to all the children had worked so hard for. Actions that will surely be met with resistance; just not at this very moment.

But that is only because the Ordermen proceed to force the rebels all the way to the center of town. Just to gather them behind the three select Ordermen that are waiting for their victims. Their molten fire irons resting in the flames as they pace back and forth with their battered faces. Demonstrating their devotion to their masters by randomly spitting out blood and twitching fervently as the adrenaline courses through their veins.

Dozens of dead and injured Ordermen line the perimeter of the fire. For such an honor surely only comes once in a lifetime. The loyalists being able to punish their leaders' arch nemeses before them is naught but a dream come true. No act of devotion could ever be greater. Yet, in order to be instilled with such honor, sacrifices must be made.

Those sacrifices force a bloodsport to form instantaneously amongst the devout Ordermen after the Top Three's announcement of the Elders' imminent approach. Talk of which spreads like wildfire amongst the mindless fools. Making it from one side of the settlement to the other in mere minutes.

While the undevout Ordermen stand there salivating over the upcoming atrocities they are about to witness, the members of The Stigmatized stand in a paralyzing state of trepidation. Bound by their hempen restraints, the rebels are forced to helplessly watch their fearless leaders be tied up before the flames. They can do naught but stand there in horror. Because they all know what torture is about to be bestowed upon them. All they can do is hope and pray that it is not taken to the extent most other beatings are—that being: to death.

To make matters worse, the Top Three make their entrance into the town square before the punishment ensues. An act that elicits thundering applause from their followers. The sound from which grows in intensity as they walk atop their wooden stage. Preaching of how they told the Elders this would happen if they ever defied their rule. As well as shaming the rebels for having fallen for their tricks. Their evil beady eyes reflecting the flames ever so devilishly as they speak.

Once the usurping trio finishes their banter, the defiant members attempt to scream over the crowd at the Top Three. Begging them to let the founding Elders go free and return things to the way they once were. But such pleas go unheard. Before they even acknowledge the rebels' existence, the three vile beings signal in unison for the torture to begin. They then turn to face the rebels. Just to crack a smile at them before turning their attention back to the flames.

The fire burns bright in the abysmal void of night. Illuminating naught but the horrid scene unfolding around it. A scene that appears to unravel from amidst the flames themselves. For that just so happens to be where the fire irons lay. Patiently waiting for their victims. Getting hotter and hotter as the moments pass. Only to scold the Elders' flesh once they are each properly fastened to the implanted wooden poles near the blaze.

Equipped with their thick leather gloves, the Ordermen hold the fire irons like baseball bats and begin repeatedly wailing on the Elders' torsos and limbs. As the men swing their molten iron rods like savages, the Elders' near-deafening cries of pain reverberate through the air. Each of which send chills down The Stigmatized members' spines. Forcing them to begin crying out louder as well. Yelling in unison for the Top Three to let them go before charging their guards with their bound bodies.

To show just how indifferent they are to the rebels' pleas and displays of courage, the Top Three allow the beating to continue for several more excruciating moments. Allowing each of the Ordermen to get in a couple more good lashings for show. Signaling for them to stop only once the Elders' cries of pain suddenly cease and their battered bodies go limp.

After the Elders' brutal fire iron lashing, the Top Three proceed to scold The Stigmatized's members. Threatening them with the same fate if they are to ever betray their rule again. Only to turn around and begin to leave a moment later. Ordering their men to rough up each of the rebels before releasing them as they mount their steeds and gallop off into the night.

Most of the rebels only get their buttocks paddled with the Ordermen's sheathed swords. But a select few are seen limping as they flee the scene. As in those with whom the Ordermen have preexisting grudges with. Even so, their punishments are nothing compared to what their mentors endured.

Luckily, the Elders manage to survive their punishment with the immediate help of their apothecary followers in The Stigmatized. Each of whom rush to the scene once the chaos disperses. With access to the restricted caches of cannabis-based healing serums that were invented before the war, it allows them to save the Elders from their inevitable death by putting them into a medically-induced comatose state with massive amounts of concentrated cannabidiol. With them having suffered several broken ribs, bones, and large portions of both second- and third-degree burns, nothing but a cannabis coma could save them. Well, a coma along with numerous healing salves and all sorts of other intimate medical care practices while they are out of commission.

In order to prevent such happenings from ever occurring again, the Elders keep to themselves after the incident. Giving themselves plenty of time to recover their battered bodies before even attempting to rehabilitate themselves. The Top Three having shown them sympathy by allowing such miraculous recoveries to occur is reason enough for them to simply fall back in line and hide in isolation. Because not only are they afraid of death themselves, they are fearful as to what The Order will do to the rest of The Stigmatized if they are to ever meet up again.

Basically, even though life returns to its normal hellish state for the defiant members, an even greater fear is bestowed upon them. That being the fear of an untimely death. One that will surely be administered in the most torturous of fashions. It is a fear that many of the rebels now come to accept as inevitable.

Yet, there are still a few younger rebels that do not seem to want to back down. Ones that continue defying The Order's laws. Each of whom get into scuffles with the Ordermen daily. Whom, in turn, gang up on them and beat the pulp out of them.

But the determined energetic youths are not deterred by such lashings. They saw what the Elders had to endure for them and feel as though they owe them something in return for such brave feats of heroism. Not to mention the tremendous contribution the Elders made to their righteous cause years before it even began. Them having nobly imparted pieces of their wisdom unto the children is what allowed them to achieve the impossible.

In turn, the young Stigmatized patriots fight with the Ordermen and create a ruckus around Fiddlers Lake every day for months. To show not only their respect for their championed Elders, but their allegiance against the Top Three as well. Displaying their Stigmatized pendants proudly as they clearly defy The Order's laws. Some even going as far as ganging up on the Ordermen and beating *them* into oblivion.

Although, such hijinks come to an abrupt stop when the Ordermen approach the Top Three to ask for permission to instill more *fear* into the young rebels. To which they willfully agree, of course. With their leaders' direct order, the Ordermen arrest all of the rebels who continually give them flak before publicly announcing that their mass execution will occur on the eve of the Autumnal Equinox in the town square.

People are furious over the announcement. They cannot wrap their heads around how their leaders could possibly justify slaying a young child. Let alone an entire group of them. It is an unprecedented event.

Primitive times or not, such punishments should never be considered against the innocent. Even the Elders muster up the courage to go up to the Top Three and plea for them to have mercy. Explaining to them a premonition they once had. One where after the first mass slaughtering of their youth, chaos will engulf the colony of survivors. An act that will ultimately cause the corrupted settlement to crumble to pieces.

However, the nefarious leadership will not give the light of day to the Elders' advice. Let alone any sort of sensible regard. They refuse to hear any propaganda but their own. Even so, they give the Elders front row access to the spectacle. Giving their victims the privilege of appearing onstage with them. Forcing them to show their disfigured selves to the curious townsfolk.

On the eve of the execution, the Top Three ignorantly stand atop their stage and watch in perverted pleasure as the young rebels are systematically slaughtered before their eyes. Except following the start of the brutal execution of their young, the citizens become outraged; just as it was forecast by the Elders. Even the Top Three's most devout followers and their own guards get stirred in with the malcontent.

Such chaos begins to erupt immediately after the leaders' vulgar display of power. Evolving quickly to the point where a group of townsfolk begin rushing the ever-growing group of Ordermen circling the stage. Each of them tries their best to break through the impenetrable mass of shielded bodies; but to no avail.

As the citizens and guards clash, the Elders sneak up from behind the Top Three and melodiously state; "We told you so."

In response, the leaders of The Order roar out in harmonious discord; "That does it the three of you! The Elders— your oh blessed Elders—are going straight to South Pass City!"

The Top Three's voices resonate through the crowds of raucous people as their words mechanically change the air around them. Their soundwaves travel through the air into everyone's tympanic membrane. Where they are ultimately transported to the cochlear and converted to vibrations in a liquid. Said vibrations are then converted by the stereocilia in one's ear into nerve impulses to be interpreted by their brain.

It is an instantaneous process that instills shock in the masses the moment the Top Three finish their fateful command. Just like that, the clashing subsides. The citizens—as well as the Ordermen—immediately turn to face the Top Three.

Upon turning their attention, the onlookers notice each of the Top Three have one of the battered Elders' necks in their left hands. Their right arms are fully extended beside them with only their index fingers pointing away; as to point toward South Pass City. A moment after their brains properly register the spectacle, harmonious gasps of horror begin resonating through the crowd. Several members of The Stigmatized nearly faint from shock over the morose announcement. Only to fully lose consciousness upon gazing at the Top Three; who proceed to toss the Elders aside. Stating they only have a single day to say their goodbyes before being sent to South Pass City to die. Just as the volunteer explorer had done years ago upon his return.

That gory return is what officially initiated the plague of fear amongst the scores of survivors years ago. Fear that still poisons each and every individual to this day. Exacerbating their insecurities to levels that the Top Three know can be exploited and pacified with harsh laws. Even if such laws mean giving up everything they hold dear, the fear-ridden survivors do not mind. They feel as though being coddled, conned, and controlled by their corrupt leaders is the only way. For if they try to go it alone out away from Fiddlers Lake, who is to say they will not also come crawling back? Only to spew up their entrails like that fated explorer had done all those years ago.

Why take such a risk when you can simply *feel* safe. Though it seems that such feelings are generally absent from those living under such harsh rule. Because apathy tends to settle in quickly when one begins believing there is nothing better.

Once such faith is lost, there is nothing one can do besides give up all hope. Unless somehow their faith is restored. Such an act being a miracle in most cases—but not now. For The Stigmatized have such miracle makers in their midst. Even if they are to be sent to their deaths tomorrow, the Elders will surely have some sort of knowledge to aid them in their predicament. At least their followers hope they do.

On their last evening in the settlement, the Elders call together one final meeting of The Stigmatized at the base of Cony Mountain. A meeting in twilight that just so happens to garner a much larger presence than any prior. Mainly because the townsfolk know they very well may never see their beloved saviors again. That fact alone is enough to make them willing to risk life and limb to hear their final words.

Although the Elders assure their followers time and time again that they will survive while giving their hours-long dramatic speeches, they themselves are not so sure. But easing their followers' minds by assuring them they have a sure-fire way of getting out of the predicament at South Pass City is the only way to keep their hopes up. Even if it is a lie, it is the only way to ensure that their allies will continue fighting for what is right.

However, the Elders are easily able to hide such lies by simply stating to their followers that they cannot divulge much deeper into their escape tactics; just in case there is another spy in their midst. For they must remain ever vigilant if they want their plans to succeed. Plans that will ultimately lead the uncorrupted away from the corrupts' settlement and back to their cavern to start fresh. Free from The Order's evil tyrannical rule.

Once they are finished assuring their followers they will survive their deaths in the morning, the Elders proceed to ask their loyal cohorts if they would like to join a new faction outside of The Order's clutches. A faction they promise will usher in a new era of luxury and peace amongst mankind. Bringing unity and fair justice back to the people. Doing so by forming a civilization for the People, by the People once again. Just as they managed to do at the beginning of The Order.

The Elders even divulge into fine details. Describing how the faction's hideout is located inside of a mountain. One that is protected on all fronts from any sort of threat that it could ever possibly face. Not to mention all of the technological luxuries inside of it that were available before the war—and then some.

People begin salivating as the Elders explain their new colony. Their eyes glazing over more and more with each passing word. As though they are each envisioning the dreamland the Elders are elaborately sketching with their words inside their mind's eye. Each mind painting its own rendition of the surreal environment as the words flow from the Elders' mouths.

Piece by piece the followers build the picture of their bright future away from The Order's dark tyranny. Only to be abruptly snapped out of such dazes once the Elders are finished speaking. For a triumphant chorus of "Aye's," begins ringing out through the air in favor of their revelation. Growing with ferocity upon hearing the new name of their faction: The Stigmata.

The Elders explain that The Stigmata stands for their marked-up flesh and broken brotherhood with The Order. They need not divulge much further. For with that simple explanation, an ear-shattering applause begins ringing out from the base of Cony Mountain. Their followers go wild with acceptance.

As they go wild, the Elders attempt to speak above the crowd. Assuring them that they will leave trails should anyone need to get away from the settlement. Something they strongly urge against. For they repeatedly tell them they will be back in a few months' time. But just in case a dire situation arises in their absence, they instruct them to follow the temporary 'S' emblems hiding amongst the greenery on the northwestern pathways. Most of which, they advise, will be destroyed after a good storm.

That is not saying making it to the new settlement will be an easy feat, either. Because the Elders go on to explain that the journey will be more grueling than anything any of them have ever experienced. Yet, they promise their followers that the rewards from their tribulations will be worth the strain.

The Stigmatized go wild with acceptance once again. Tears begin streaming down random people's faces. All while others scream with joy. Only for such ruckus to suddenly cease upon the Elders' signal. Them each raising their hands before taking turns speaking; "Good luck and God speed. Shall we for some unforeseeable reason not make it past this inexcusable punishment tomorrow, we will see you all on the other side."

After they finish their fond farewell, the Elders bow before the crowd of jovial followers. All of whom cheer and parade around the trio before allowing them to hastily proceed back to their cabins. Because they all know there are hordes of Ordermen awaiting their arrival. The raucous sounds of celebration and death heard in the distance guarantee such facts.

In order to pass the time, the Ordermen begin celebrating in the only way they know how: with violence. Going so far as beginning a tournament-style sword-fighting competition in front of the Elders' cabins beneath the brilliant night sky while waiting for their return. Maiming and killing one another in the process.

Lifeless and limbless bodies are periodically dragged out of the ring of spectating bodies. Each one leaving behind pungent trails of scarlet carnage. They wait so long and the crowd gets so large that blood begins puddling atop the saturated earthen paths leading to their homes. Making quite a sight for the wary tenants.

Upon their arrival, some of the Ordermen mock the Elders. Others slash at their flesh with their blades. The rest make threatening gestures toward them with their torches. All before ultimately letting the Elders proceed into their cabins unscathed. Doing so just to hinder their founders' slumber that much more. As to ensure they have ethereal nightmares of the brutal death they are about to endure in just a few faithful hours.

Unfortunately, sleep never comes for the Elders. With all of their fears overburdening their minds, how could it? Instead, they rise from their raised feathered mattresses before dawn to the sound of Ordermen busting through each of their cabin doors. Just to be dragged from their place of slumber and out the door.

Such is a fitting way for anyone to start their final day. At least to the selected Ordermen it is. Because for them, today is the day they earn the most respect an Orderman will ever receive. Today they get to abolish their leaders' main adversaries. Removing those thorns from their sides—once and for all. A deed only those select few Ordermen will ever be able to accomplish. With that being the case, the Top Three have a few of their youngest, most loyal and trusted servants do such a bidding. Each of whom are ecstatic to be granted such an honor. The three of them having a lifetime to gloat over such achievements and all.

The selected Ordermen let such honor be known, too. For upon exiting the cabins, they begin relentlessly jabbing the Elders with their sheathed blades. Forcing them to walk for miles with such incessant prodding. Yet, luck appears to be on the Elders' side. Seeing as how their trek is mostly downhill, it makes the cruelty a tad bit easier to avoid. If they do manage to make contact though, the Ordermen make sure each prod is felt. A feat they accomplish by jabbing their sheathed blades multiple times into the Elders' lower back with short yet powerful thrusts.

However, the Elders use their smarts to try and outmaneuver the youthful Ordermen. Bobbing, weaving, and hustling so much that by ten o'clock in the morning, they reach the outskirts of South Pass City. A time in which the Elders' freshly concocted plans begin coming to fruition.

The group keeps going until they reach the peak of the highlands overlooking South Pass City. Before them are naught but deserted valleys below. Death on all fronts. Yet, a polychromatic veil is visible in the distance. Complete with a resonant hum emanating forth from its radiant beauty.

Just outside of the veil lays dense greenery. Vines on top of vines. Trees so massive they block out the sun all around them and create large patches of ominous void. Each of which conceal whatever other sorts of life are stirring within their depths.

Sporadic assortments of ginormous flowers of all kinds blossom amongst the overwhelming amounts of exposed foliage. Surely housing insects and other animals just as massive in size. If only the group could visibly make them out from their distance. But that is entirely unnecessary. Because the sight of the foliage alone is enough for them to completely lose their minds. The bizarre sight paralyzes each of their beings. Forcing them to stand and stare for so long they forget just why they are even there.

At the peak the saintly victims and their oblivious executioners silently stand. Each of them completely flabbergasted by the sudden transition before their eyes. That being the lack of life preceding copious amounts of it. Separated by naught but the humming multicolored veil before them.

As they stand there, the Ordermen begin observing the terrain beneath them. Only to soon notice the skeletal remains of one of the volunteer exploration teams. All of whose bones are broken and randomly scattered roughly a half mile below. Appearing as though they have been blown to pieces by the monstrosity lurking below. Whatever the veil is, it is surely what laid waste to the dead. *Nothing* outside of their young and feeble minds can explain otherwise. Meaning they must act fast.

After seeing the chaotically strewn remains of the fallen, the Ordermen suddenly snap back to reality. Without a second thought, they each unholster and proceed to load the revolvers the Top Three gave them for their mission. However, with such ominous sights pinging through their minds and death possibly feet away, their cortisol starts flowing in response. Their hands begin shuddering as they fill their gun's chambers with bullets and ready them to fire. Making the premeditated scene they had thought would strike fear into their victims' souls become naught but a display of their true cowardice.

Several tense moments pass as the Ordermen fumble to load their guns. Only for them to dutifully point them at the Elders before proceeding to bicker amongst themselves. Moments later, one of the youths barks out the order for the Elders to go on ahead. A strong sensation of fear begins diffusing through the air as the Orderman starts to speak. It is one that can be felt all throughout each of their beings. As though it is being cast out by the veil before them. Moments later, his words are cut off by a volume spike in the incessant humming; completely halting his speech.

The deafening sound forces the group to cover their ears in response. Making it clearly evident that they are all well beyond their point of comfort. The youths more so than the Elders; them nearly dropping their guns in the process of blocking the sudden noise proves such facts.

Seeing that their predicament is beginning to play out in their favor, the Elders begin taking advantage of the youths' fear. Doing so by simply proceeding onwards. A time in which they procure a brilliant idea. One they know will completely shatter the Ordermen's feeble minds and get them out of their dilemma; hopefully once and for all. Because if their plan works, their executioners will certainly report them as dead to their corrupt masters; as to protect their own hides. Freeing them from the bonds of tyranny for the rest of their days.

The Elders' plan is simple. As soon as they take their first step, the trio will begin acting erratically. Screaming out in pain before dropping to the ground and writhing in agony. Essentially pulling a Dahmer and feign seizing. Acting like clowns in order to scare their executioners.

Their theory is that once the Ordermen see the Elders' plight occurring so close to them, no matter how ridiculous it may seem, they will immediately hightail it out of there. Just like the cowards they truly are. Running away whilst screaming like little sissy babies the entire way. Because they may be able to force death and suffering onto others, but when it comes to themselves, the youths will be unable to face such fates and will do anything to escape.

Such theories become facts almost immediately after the Elders' rendition. Minutes later, once the Ordermen are long gone, they hightail it out of there as well. Chuckling as they periodically jest amongst themselves over their cleverness. Those random bits of joy last the entire duration of their northwest trek to their new home. Each bit strengthening their resolve to endure.

Now, traversing treacherous terrain can be a hassle for anyone. But, one's ability to cope and recover continually gets worse with age. This is particularly so when one does not exercise their body regularly. Even if they do, once one has had their bones broken and their bodies battered by maniacal madmen, they still require a lot of time to recover. Meaning the fire iron lashing the Elders suffered five months ago makes their task of covering forty miles of rugged terrain all at once that much harder. Especially when they have been pushing themselves all morning.

Now, endurance most certainly does not come easy to an untrained body. Them having been cooped up in a cabin for months trying to rehabilitate does not help the Elders' case at all. Neither does their hurried ten-mile trek toward the southern barrier, which took quite a toll on the trio. A fact that becomes apparent to the aged men once they rise from the ground to begin their twelve-mile trek back toward the settlement. Forcing them to confront the fact that they are not spring chickens anymore.

Even so, the Elders manage to keep their spirits up. Their scheduled rest stop at Cony Mountain being the incentive. For they go there to pick up supplies left by their loyal followers. Such being several full canteens of fresh water; a few finely crafted bows and bladed weapons; as well as insulated apparel and pairs of rubber-soled boots. Even though they did leave foodstuffs, it seems as though some scavenging beasts picked through them overnight. Meaning they must ration what is left.

While trying to keep their over-active minds occupied during the final stretch of their perilous eighteen-mile journey to Mount Chauvenet, the Elders make trail markers out of sticks and vines. They fashion 'S' insignias out of the foliage and start hanging them from every fifth tree. Providing any of the unfortunate Fiddlers Lake escapees with the guidance symbols they had promised them the night before. Doing so as they huff and puff their way through the treacherous landscape. Stopping only twice to refuel and rest their weary bodies.

By midnight of the same night, cold, battered, and beaten by their surrounding elements, the Elders reach Mount Chauvenet. Upon confronting the lair's entrance, one of the Elders roar out the mysterious password; "Aperi que ostian nunc," before a veil cloaked amidst the cliff face begins to lift. Revealing a secret entrance into the mountain several feet above them.

Once the veil fully exposes the dark depths of the cavern's entrance above, a set of stone stairs begin protruding out from the cliff face diagonally from it. Rocks drop from above and the earth moves below as the stairs individually, yet uniformly expose themselves. As they inch outwards, they effortlessly clear their path of any debris. Just to come to a sudden stop a few feet later.

Out from the cliff a set of three-foot-wide by one-foot-long and two-inch-deep steps are born; each one independent of the other. With only an inch separating them, the steps make the Elders trek into the exposed mouth of the cavern effortless. It also causes them to completely lose their composure over the mystifying series of events. Their emotions run absolutely wild. Nostalgia begins flooding their beings and shortly thereafter, tears begin trickling down their bearded faces as they start ascending the stairs.

Upon reaching the entrance, the Elders race into the deepest and darkest depths of the caverns to see the marvels of their preprogrammed work. As they advance forward through the narrowing entranceway, they come to a platform connected to a ramp leading to the bottom of the cave. Their presence causes a series of lights to begin illuminating their path down. Only to find their very own personalized cabins awaiting their arrival at the bottom of the now brightly lit cavern.

It soon becomes clear that all is going according to the Elders' plan. With everything seemingly well under way, it becomes quite apparent to them that now is the time to initiate their ultimate goal. That being: to begin a perfect society inside of Mount Chauvenet. A society void of any of the Malentians' corrupt drones.

For months after their arrival, the Elders prepare the caverns for the influx of people. Tinkering and toiling with the high-tech toys they had left behind many years ago. However, there is not much shelter-wise to prepare. Only workings of luxury are to be hashed out and put into action by this point.

One must realize that the Elders want to blow the pants off their new recruits and show them that there truly is a heavenly paradise at the end of their years of suffering. You see, the Elders have their own secret laboratory inside of the cavern. A lab where they can print and make anything they can imagine. So, they utilize such a lab to design new inventions for their residents; printing nonstop for months on end to bring them to life. Finally, after years of suffering, the Elders are able to bring their bottled-up thoughts to fruition and satiate their inventive minds.

Once they have satisfied their lust for creation, the Elders are ready to proceed forth with their hunt for pure blood. With their new technology in tow, they are able to hide themselves with mystical cloaks fashioned from various metamaterials. Making it possible for them to sneak through the settlement undetected.

To ensure their secrecy as well as their integrity, the Elders spread the word to the prior Stigmatized leaders in the most obnoxious way possible. A feat they accomplish by rehearsing the same mystical act amongst themselves to perfection before visiting the same three leaders that visited them the night of their return. Committing acts of reverse déjà vu when each of them go in solo to confront their youthful apprentices.

On the eve of the customary weeks-long winter celebration is when the Elders choose to visit. That being the night before the Ordermen spend the year's final weeks eating and getting wasted off the spirits made from the harvest of the year prior. The Top Three being the hosts of such events. Them showing up in the dead of night at the foot of the youths' beds is an act that would most certainly merit alarm for any citizen at Fiddlers Lake.

When the Elders proceed to wake the three young leaders by means of tickling their feet, they wake from their slumber ready to meet a dire fate. Upon becoming cognizant and realizing their predicament is not as dire as they had anticipated, each of the rebellious youths nearly has an infarction over the unbelievable sight. One of their esteemed Elders standing before them is miraculous. It is also far more relieving than waking up to a drunken pack of Ordermen looking to start the celebration early. Of whom would more likely than not beat them into oblivion before slaughtering them and feeding their hacked-up corpse to the livestock; or to the townsfolk themselves if they so please.

Before the Stigmatized leaders can speak and cause any sort of ruckus, the Elders finish the enactment of their brief rehearsed scene. Doing so by quietly hushing their apprentice before asking them to relay their vital message to the rest of the wannabe defectors. Each of them giving the exact same instructions:

"Gather everyone together for one last excursion in a week's time. If you all sneakily depart on the eve of the solstice, The Order will never dare follow. Simply trek twenty miles northwest utilizing the Wind River Range as guidance. Continue following the mountains until you reach Little Valentine Lake. It is there you will find your paradise."

After they present their message, the Elders take a bow in order to inconspicuously set a rolled-up map at the foot of their apprentice's bed. Upon standing upright once more, they suddenly vanish. Cloaking themselves before disappearing into the night. Making the leaders unsure as to whether it was truly one of the Elders, or just a ghastly bode of dissociation.

Still, The Stigmatized manages to secretly converge at a randomly selected spot around Cony Mountain the following afternoon. Only for them to almost immediately come to the conclusion that the visions were no happenstance. Seeing as how the Elders had given each of them the exact same message, it is hard not to believe. Not to mention the identical printed maps they each received. Maps that have the entire Wind River Range scrawled out meticulously all the way up to Grand Teton National Park.

The Elders even leave a—barely visible—smudge right around Little Valentine Lake in order to steer their followers in the right direction. A smudge that, when viewed closely, has a clear 'S' embossed in its center. Seeing such an inconspicuous, yet helpful clever hint instantly vanquishes the members' doubts into both the maps' and the messengers' authenticity.

With all three maps being identical, there is no doubt in anyone's mind that it was anyone but their beloved Elders that sent the message. For they are the only ones capable of scribing such meticulous pieces of art. Especially if they have found the mystical caverns they spoke so highly of on that fateful night three months ago. One that suddenly seems like yesterday.

Even though a few months have passed, the moment they finally converge again to discuss the event, time suddenly stops for The Stigmatized members. Déjà vu is definitely sensed at their meeting. Because the last time any of them have felt any semblance of such relief was during the Elders' final speech. A speech that, to their followers, seemed to be just another spot-on premonition. One which is now unfolding before their eyes.

Sure enough, as the group hashes out their plans of escape to a point of perfection during their final week, it becomes an iconic moment in human history. All of the surreal events that have transpired up to this point are iconic in the Elders' followers' eyes—miracles even. The climactic point around Cony Mountain is just icing on the cake. In an instant, life changes for The Stigmatized members. On that fateful day, lives that would otherwise end dull and dreary suddenly turn in the people's favor.

Their saviors' simple instructions are all the downtrodden rebels need to become lively once more. With their rejuvenated souls, people start heading out of Fiddlers Lake in droves. Beginning such dangerous endeavors on winter solstice eve. Just as the Elders had commanded.

Winter solstice eve is one unlike any other during the weeks-long celebration. Not only does it precede the year's longest night, it also marks the start of The Order's renowned Yuletide festival. A time in which gift-giving and brown-nosing are all the rage. With that being the case, the rebels have to be extra careful during their escape.

In order to evade detection, The Stigmatized separates their faction into three groups. Each of which take different routes out of the lake to ensure at least one of them makes it out alive. With all of the paths out of the settlement being patrolled by Ordermen, there is no such thing as being too cautious.

Although that is *normally* the case, the Ordermen are well beyond the point of sober by nightfall on the eve of this solstice. Nearly all of them are gathered in the town square partying with the Top Three. Making the rebels' escape that much simpler.

After they all make it out of the settlement, the groups rendezvous at Tayo Park. Where they proceed to follow the mountains to Mount Chauvenet and then to Little Valentine Lake. Just as the Elders had stated during their ghastly appearance.

The Stigmatized's escape from Fiddlers Lake goes down in The Order's books as a shameful event marked by scores of precautionary failures. Once they fully come to realize what has happened, there is no way they can ever go back to the way things were. Because shortly after the initial escape, scores of others follow suit. Meaning they must label such disastrous events with the proper moniker. That being: The Great Mutiny.

When word of a colony in the mountains with technology begins spreading throughout Fiddlers Lake, people cannot help but defect from its hellish conditions. Especially since the remaining uncorrupted are now the minorities. They are the corrupts' biological enemies. Enemies that cannot even begin to stand up to their oppressors because they have been relentlessly conditioned otherwise. A conditioning that becomes all the more exacerbated and wide-spread after such defections.

How is the populace being conditioned, you may be asking? Well, since the Top Three took over Fiddlers Lake, they have been adamant in their plans to dehumanize their citizens. As to make sure feelings of helplessness are engrained in each and every one of them.

If you do so recall, amidst the confusion after the Elders' initial disappearance, the Top Three's seeds were sown within the confines of the settlement. Just days after their founders' vanishing, the oppressive regime had begun beating down the people's self-esteem and molding them into apathetic slaves to do their bidding. With the sudden overzealous promotion of spirits and other fermented beverages in the following weeks, it soon became clear what sort of foul treachery had begun brewing.

Seeing as how alcohol has never not been readily available amongst the survivors, most of them simply choose to do naught but drink away their misery. Such soul-crushing factors are elevated with the induction of pubs, which are used to engage in those addictive and depressing social activities. All of which are sporadically built throughout the settlement. Gerrymandered to the point of perfection in the Top Threes' eyes. As to assure patrons with favorable allegiance toward them greatly outnumber those without.

This makes it impossible for any sort of insurrection to ever be hashed out within the walls of said establishments. For with the many mindless prying ears present, along with the constant need for glory amongst their tyrant masters, no one dares to speak of such blasphemy. Lest they wish to be immediately dragged to the town square and beaten to death like all the others.

In days long past, pubs were used to sow the seeds of revolution. This much is true. However, in today's dismal environment, no such revolts are even whispered. Pubs are now a place where people go to dwell on their own self-pity and lack of control. This being due to the realization by the people that there really may not be anywhere else on the planet they can escape to. It may very well be humanity's last stand.

One would think with those dire straits being the case, they would cause an internal savage reaction against one's hostile environment in order for them to both survive and strive. But with such depressants flowing freely, and the untrustworthiness present amongst them, the downtrodden citizens do naught but whine and moan. Crying within their own hearts and souls while trying to appear normal during social time with their peers. Imbibing on spirits while inadvertently destroying their own.

With such cowardice present amongst the majority of the herd, everyone that is not in that majority becomes suspect. Meaning each person that dares to be an individual is held accountable for their nonconformist ways. To ensure the rest of the disobedient stay in line, the Ordermen make *examples* of every so many rebels they punish. Preaching that it is for the safety of the herd to calm the innocent bystanders present during said random acts.

That being because maintaining a conformist status amongst said herd is a must during such times of deceit. The last thing someone wants is to be deemed suspicious by a neighbor or a loyalist frenemy. Especially since such spineless acts become gravely exacerbated with the sudden influx of free pubs around the lake shortly after The Great Mutiny.

After the defection, the Top Three have to think of ways to appease those they still have under their control. Retardants have worked well thus far; they just need to amplify their effects. To do so, they have the Ordermen construct several more pubs in each of the segregated territories. As well as lessen the punishments given to those willing to speak out against them. If lessened but more frequent punishments do not appease, then the mandatory activity of congregating to deliberately dumb themselves down several times per week must suffice.

To ensure their success in devolving the population, The Order outlaws cannabis and all other hallucinogenic drugs. You know, the ones that actually help the human brain evolve and regenerate. That way people are only able to kill brain cells instead of repair and maintain them. Forever hindering their critical thinking skills and diminishing their overall health.

Yet, with free coping mechanisms (addictive liquids) flowing at all times of the day throughout the settlement, who could care less about such depressing states; let alone pass up such opportunities? Especially when the Top Three make the curfew a thing of the past. All while introducing more distractions for the masses—such as gambling and sports.

That is not saying there are not any drawbacks to such *liberating* policies though. Because to ensure that no one else ever escapes, the Top Three construct watchtowers every quarter mile around the perimeter of their expansive settlement. Forcing **all** of the Ordermen to stand guard 24/7 in order to catch any vile defectors and bring them back into their crooked society.

Even with all of the preventative actions taken during The Top Three's first year in charge, over three-quarters of the colony manages to escape. Only leaving The Order's closest and most loyal members behind. A number of loyalists that quickly grows to be well in the thousands over the years. Because misery loves company and all that hullabaloo. Well, not only that. The corrupted must stick together to sustain their entropic ways.

But still, what kind of corrupt mind would ever turn down the opportunity to instill fear into an entire colony of humans? Most certainly none of the ones at Fiddlers Lake. They dedicate their entire lives to engaging in such grotesque displays of power. With not a care in the world for those they inflict their evil onto.

Even those that get cast out to Death Valley do not think of fleeing. For with the introduction of pubs, cabin homes, slave labor (*jobs*), and Ordermen-kept farmlands, life becomes a lot less burdensome for the outcasts. Although the Ordermen wail on the citizens every time they come around, the citizens have naught a care in the world with the liquid spirits coursing through their veins. How can one possibly care when they are constantly numb both internally and externally?

In regards to controlling a populace, alcohol is definitely the drug of choice. Seeing as how it *is* a highly addictive depressant that affects both body and mind, tyrannical rulers do not need much else. Because it effectively takes its user on a dark euphoric roller coaster of a ride that gets them hooked and fiending for more after only the first few doses. Them having the need to drink liquids anyway makes the poisonous one a wonderful substitute. Hell, it gets you drunk.

That is not saying this *drunk* does not have its consequences. This being because the popular ride has the potential to poison one's body to death. Overdoses are quite common amongst the forlorn. There not being any set limit for the patrons guarantees such outcomes.

If the user does not allow their body to filter out and process the poisonous liquid accordingly, as in binge drinking, the greater the percentage of it circulating through their bloodstream will be. So will their likelihood of experiencing a hormonal imbalance. This being due to the fact that most fermented beverages contain xenoestrogens, which mimic the female sex hormone, estrogen.

As if all of those factors were not bad enough, alcohol has the potential to completely inhibit one's ability to function. But only when they choose to imbibe too much. Once one manages to reach a blood alcohol content of less than a mere half of a percent, they are nearly guaranteed a grave. Unless their body impulsively expels the poison, of course. That is not even touching upon its lethal withdrawal process. Not to mention what all else it does to aid in the degradation of one's body over time with continued use.

With alcohol being the only legal drug, it is no wonder as to why the remaining bunch of civilians manage to stay loyal to The Order. They simply do not care what goes on around them. As long as they can get their fix, everything is right in their eyes.

Such sad states of affairs are just how the Malentians want it, too. Because if you do not step outside of your own little box and gather information about the world around you, you are not really living. You are simply existing and playing into their wanton system of apathetic living. Making no noticeable impact on the world.

With one's motivation sapped away by booze and their self-esteem obliterated on a daily basis by The Order's army, there is really no hope for the downtrodden. All it takes is a year after The Great Mutiny for people to become complete prisoners to their unscrupulous overlords. By that time though, no one dares to even think of leaving either Death Valley or Fiddlers Lake.

You see, with the entire perimeter of the settlement now guarded 24/7 by armed guards, there really is no escape. The people are basically trapped there until they die. A death the

Ordermen can induce instantaneously if their foul hearts do so desire. Seeing as how it is *their* land and *they* are the law.

With the combination of strict law and an entire army of mindless, yet brutal enforcers, the people at The Order's settlements are destined for misery. Such a combination is no good for any sort of stable civilization. Because for it to be a stable civilization, one's rulers must practice civility. Over half of civility is in civilization for flark's sake. They apparently go hand in hand. Not to mention the fact that a state of entropy will eventually reach equilibrium if left to itself.

No such practices are to ever be enforced by those corrupt with the Malentians' evil though. Acts of civility are nowhere to be found amongst their kind. Not even in the darkest depths of their soul. The evil resonates deep within. Eventually, it completely consumes its host. But only once it has complete control of their empty shell of a mind. Because the corrupt are the weakest and most spineless humans on the face of the Earth.

It does not take much to deny said evil's foul temptations. Some people just want to watch the world be smothered to oblivion it seems. Even though it does not take much resistance to deny the evil entirely, it takes less to accept it. To embrace it. To let it take complete control of your being. Of course, a lot of humans choose the latter due to the fact they do not believe in themselves. They would rather live in a state of perpetual evil based on ignorance and belief than defect and educate themselves. All before dismissing said state's foul ways and abandoning it altogether. Just like The Stigmatized did during The Great Mutiny.

Those that still had an ounce of decency in them and chose to defect in the beginning of it all did so bravely. Even though the consequences of being caught in such acts was certain death, people took the Elders' bait and finally freed themselves from their oppressive chains to begin anew in the mountains. Forever eluding the corrupt Top Three and their wretched hellish society. Because a life of freedom is worth far more than a life of secure suffering brought on by a few wicked men.

Now, there are still people after The Great Mutiny who manage to flee and find salvation away from the corrupt. Even so, they are only able to escape the settlement before the watchtowers are built. Because such a feat becomes next to impossible once they are erected.

Overall, the people who manage to escape Fiddlers Lake after The Great Mutiny do so at their own peril and with little guidance; that they are aware of at least. All to try and find salvation with the others that defected before them. Those honest people are picked up and taken in by The Stigmata with open arms. Most of them are just innocent citizens after all. They are simply afraid of what The Order has become. As well as afraid of what might have happened to their families if they had stayed any longer.

That is not saying The Stigmata have not had their fair share of imitators. Yes, the Ordermen have tried to breach their ranks many times. However, every time they have failed. Mainly due to the fact that the Elders invented special eyewear to detect whether or not one is corrupted by the Malentians' evil.

Even though such technology was given to them by the Sagacians, the Elders have no need to tell the others. Who would believe them anyway? With the Elders' history of achievements, their supporters believe they are capable of anything. Them having ushered in a great deal of the technological wonders of the past and all.

With such technology in their midst, patrolling Stigmatamen are able to detect corrupted beings and slay them on the spot. Utilizing what appear to be a pair of cheap sunglasses to complete such tasks. Seeing as how all of the defectors are directed to Little Valentine Lake before discovering the entrance to their bunker, the Stigmatamen are easily able to do their job.

As if the Stigmatamen having the ability to instantly decipher friend from foe is not easy enough, with their laser guns stationed atop Cathedral Peak, their job is a piece of cake. All they have to do is point a tracker at their target and *bang*. Job done. Even when there are corrupt beings present, the sudden flash of light that immediately follows their detection is barely noticeable. The only thing the others really see is a body falling to the ground. Making it appear as though the corrupt being simply keeled over from exhaustion. Their fall being what causes the blood to pour from their skull. At least that is what the innocent ones are led to believe.

Once they are deemed safe, the refugees are welcomed into The Stigmata with open arms. With such protective measures in place, the Elders' perfect colony begins flourishing. Not only are many of the surviving warriors who fought in The Great Bio War and their families a part of their ranks, there are also scores of young dissenters from Fiddlers Lake and Death Valley. All of whom truly despise the heinous ways of The Order. Some going so far as leaving their loved ones behind to escape the tyranny.

No matter how hard it may be, the dissenters know such painful separations must occur for their own good. For there is no one else but you to trust with your own fate. Especially when faced with dire straits that have the propensity to prematurely end your life. Such as when one simply acts out in any other manner besides the one in which they are directed.

At Fiddlers Lake the dissenters that are so open-handedly taken in by The Stigmata come to be known as *Mutineers*. Even to this day every Mutineer has a bounty on their head. If any of them are seen, they are to be executed on sight. Rewards are to be given on a per corpse basis.

Unfortunately for them, only one of the Mutineers ever manages to get caught. That being one who failed in freeing his brainwashed family. For who needs to leave the confines of a cavern with every possible amenity a human could ever ask for? That simple fact drives the Top Three mad. Never being able to punish the *wicked* drives them to the brink of insanity. So much so that they vow to find the Mutineers' new location and exterminate every single scum sucking one of them. Because if you are not under their rule, you are not under the right rule—and that is *that*!

Enough of the doom and gloom. Let us now move back to The Stigmata. You see, The Stigmata view everyone as family. They are one giant family with naught but trust and civility amongst their ranks. Meaning the atmosphere inside of their cavernous hideout is just as it was before the Elders had left in the beginning of The Order. Except now their living conditions are in tune with what they were before the war. Just with stone surrounding them instead of sky. The latter of which is readily accessible whenever they wish.

Each family has their own cabin complete with electricity, heat, and fresh water. There are jobs for everyone as well. But only if that is how they wish to pass the time. For there is a line of shops and marketplaces along the base of the cavern where people go to get nourishment produced and goods distributed by both humans and autonomous beings. Of whom work side-by-side to utilize the foods and goods donated by the more generous and crafty families to provide for the rest of the caverns. That is not even mentioning the assortment of print-on-demand goods for sale by folks in their cabins throughout the cave.

Goods crafted by members of The Stigmata themselves are used to barter. A system that soon catches on amongst the pure-hearted Stigmata members. Since everyone is capable of independently supporting and defending themselves, no other system is necessary. If they want something from someone, they simply supply whatever demand is requested. If no demand is to be had, they try to create it. When all else fails, they donate their work in the hopes that someone finds some use for it. Forcing them to both think and socialize outside of the box to get their products or skills some traction.

Apart from the shops along the base of the cavern is the town square, which is where people come to gather and eat. Just as a family should. Not only do they eat, they socialize as well. Arranging and throwing weekly birthday parties to highlight and celebrate their members' lives; as well as their freedom from tyranny. Making sure they let such freedoms be known. A task that is made simple with everyone living so close to one another.

Along the sides of the walls of the cavern, above the shops, are several rows of cabins. Each of which are nearly identical in size; just not in appearance. That being because members of The Stigmata are free to customize them as they please. To aid in such tasks, each of them are provided with their own computer and 3D printing device. Giving them the ability to research, create, and print almost anything their minds desire. Allowing many new brainchildren to be brought to life.

Less tech savvy folks, or those just looking for a professional's input, just have to describe what they want to the online community and voila! It appears at their doorstep the next day. Sometimes even the same day. Such being dependent on their ability to supply either work or another item in return. As well as the others' current workload or interest into such matters.

The atmosphere is downright ethereal compared to what the people have already grown accustomed to after the war. Each of them knows it is truly a miracle that such a place exists during these troubled times. They know that for a fact and are willing to sacrifice life and limb to protect it.

In order to protect their newfound lifestyle, everyone in the cavern trains. All Stigmata members are molded into fearless warriors. Not only are they warriors, they are survivors as well. For their very lives depend on it when they traverse the ranges.

Due to such facts, everyone has their choice of weaponry and are thoroughly trained on how to properly use all of them. From laser guns to bow and arrows, knives to spears, they master them all. Because not only do they have to defend the caves, they all still have to hunt for their survival too. Entire families traverse through the mountains and valleys to hunt, fish, and camp.

Parents educate their children at a young age. Teaching them how to both scavenge and survive out in the wilderness. Just as it was at Fiddlers Lake and how it should be anywhere. Hunting, fishing, cooking, as well as planting and harvesting are just some of the basics the children know by the age of ten.

To ensure their safety, children are thoroughly trained in close combat as well. They are also knowledgeable when it comes to emergency medical procedures and overall basic survival skills out in the wilderness. That way if anything happens, each family's members will know exactly what to do with little guidance. These skills make it easier to cope when those inevitable events occur. But even when faced with such strife, life will remain golden knowing what is waiting for them back home.

With everyone instantly being on the same page when a disaster strikes, every excursion is a fruitful one. A fact that shows. For every Stigmata family that goes out comes back bearing more than they are able to carry. Even when things do manage to go south, the groups manage to stack resources atop their injured companion. Tying bags of herbs and fruits to the sides of their makeshift stretchers; if they are so injured. Utilizing everything they can to make up for the lost set of hands. Because with a continuously growing number of mouths to feed, every family needs to do all they can to fend for their cavernous Stigmata family.

It does not take long for the Elders to transform the caves into a harmonious city in the deepest, darkest parts of Mount Chauvenet. Throughout the years, the caverns continue to change; to evolve. Bringing forth massive shops complete with all sorts of hand-made commodities by the craftier of folks; eateries with sit-in eating, as well as speedy service; and even an armory complete with the latest and greatest weaponry printed up by the Elders themselves.

Humanity flourishes and evolves in the caves. As stated before, The Stigmata members protect their sanctuary with their lives. To further ensure their success, groups of rogue hunters are deployed by the Elders. All of whom scour the outlying ranges surrounding Mount Chauvenet. Not only for food, but for signs of human life.

You see, the Elders have a very simple plan. After their new civilization begins to blossom, they plan to have patrols amidst every mountain just waiting for the arrival of the prophetic *Chosen*. All of whom are to ascend from Fiddlers Lake; as it has been foretold. These Chosen are the *Warriors of Sight* spoken of in the ancient Judex Sapiens' lore. In which fabled heroes are to come forth from a lake and bring life on Earth back to the way it was before the Malentians' meddling. Doing so by vanquishing the evil that plagues the Universe. Something that will surely be a feat in and of itself.

They are also to be the last of the Mutineers coming from said lake. Escaping only to find salvation elsewhere. Away from the plague of darkness at the lake that inevitably overcomes the minds of the Malentians' puppets. There is just one tiny oversight though: no one knows exactly when this will occur.

These *Last Mutineers* are the only ones capable of leaving the Sagacians' force field. They are also the only ones with the unfathomable skills to conquer the prerequisite tasks necessary to accomplish such a feat. Only to travel hundreds of miles down south to a secret government facility in New Mexico immediately after. A facility housing a top-secret portal that will take them to the dimension in which the Sagacians are currently residing.

Once they cross into their alien world, the Chosen will have the opportunity to work with the Sagacians. But only to formulate a plan and restore the Universe to its former glory. One that focuses on destroying their Malentian adversaries and freeing the Judex Sapiens from captivity.

However kooky it sounds, that lore is preached night and day by the Elders to their loyal followers. Still, they never really divulge too deep into where exactly they get their information from. Meaning it is definitely a hard pill for some to swallow. Especially coming from their blessed idols, who are the very reason they are all alive today.

Even with the Elders' lunatic preaching, the people begin to settle down and become content with their new living arrangements. As time seemingly flies by, it all starts to seem as though it is too perfect to be true—and that may very well be the case. For only the trio knows why things are going so well.

Yes, the Elders have a dark secret that they know can only be told to those Chosen few. A secret that has been passed down since the first generation of Judex Sapiens populated the Universe several googolplexes ago. Making it the best kept secret of all time. For if the Malentians were to ever get word of the secret, they would surely use it to end all life in an instant.

Although it has been nearly two decades since The Great Mutiny, the Elders' spirits still remain high. They continue to preach their alien lore night and day. Speaking to the Sagacians every chance they can by fishing for sturgeons in Valentine Lake. Simply hoping to hear some good news about the prophecy.

With them running out of time on this Earth, you would think the Sagacians would at least tell the Elders *something*. Instead, they do naught but insist that it is only a matter of time. Promising them that the ominous breeze they can feel wafting throughout the valley is no happenstance. Because the Chosen's awakening is finally upon us...

Patrick Michael Anthony Bedont Jr.
† ◊ ∞ ‡ 14 Words ‡ ∞ ◊ †

Patrick Bedont Jr. is a simple man that hails from a small town in southwestern Pennsylvania. Being birthed into a White family showed Patrick that hard work and dedication will only get you so far. For it is all about (((who))) you know in today's economy that will get you anywhere. Else you are destined for a life of debt slavery. Slaving for the (((corporations))) for mediocre wages that slowly decline over the years as (((inflation))) runs rampant in a world economy that consists of naught but valueless (((fiat))) currencies. No longer can a family get by with one sole provider. Those days are long gone. Instead, both parents have to work to just barely make ends meet. Such truths have effectively transformed humanity into generations of conquered (((usury))) slaves yet again. By forgetting history, we have repeated it.

We have let a select (((cabal))) of *humans* degenerate our species back to the fall of ancient Rome. Just like back then, all we have to rely on in our White Republic is what little hope we have left in a system that has rewarded naught but the (((wealthy))) to somehow reverse such trends. Never will these *men* reverse the atrocities they wreak on mankind as long as they are endlessly filling their pockets with currencies on our behalf. Sure, the idea of trickle-down economics sounds good on paper. But when the wealth is left in the hands of the (((greedy))) corrupt, there is little we as tax cattle can do except hope our elected officials do what we elect them to do: represent us.

Something that does not look like it will start happening any time soon. At least not with the **bribes** disguised as *campaign contributions* flowing through our (((corrupted))) system. Along with the unlimited congressional terms presently demonstrated. Both of which do naught but create (((government))) lifers that get to retire on the taxpayers' dime after spending a lifetime fucking them over.

Patrick is afraid that if we do not take drastic measures, our European species does not stand much of a chance on this blessed sphere much longer. That is why he started writing the fantasy series titled, *The Last Mutineers*. Writing in the simple hopes that, through the power of literature and imagination, perhaps he will be able to persuade his fellow Americans into changing their despondent ways by showing them there is a light at the end of the diversity tunnel. Because even with such an oppressive government towering over our nation, we still have the freedom of speech; (((for the most part.))) We also have the entire world's knowledge at our fingertips. Just imagine if people used it to train their mind instead of using it to view garbage propaganda.

But alas, we as a species have been subjected to another Dark Age at the hands of our governing bodies. These governments *are* intertwined with the central banksters. All of whom conspire with their corporate cronies to bring about the downfall of the civilized world. Doing so by taking over the education systems while distracting the masses with mindless media. Diversifying their lands in order to divide them over matters of race and religion. It is a sad state of affairs in this world. Affairs we are all forced to endure against our will. So, it is up to authors like Patrick to address these topics and get people thinking outside of their comfort margins.

Not until we *all* begin rising up and taking our power back will things change. With the treasonous media distracting the masses with the happenings of celebrities instead of those of our representatives, I fear we are doomed. Especially with the media being able to effectively utilize one of the most ancient strategies of war—divide and conquer— on the ignorant masses, we do not stand a chance. For the longer we stay divided, the easier it will be for them to control us completely.

With the police-state mentality and political correctness flowing freely, forever impeding our sovereignty, it is just a matter of time before it all implodes. Because when such ignorant mindsets become prevalent throughout a Republic, it only takes a bit of time before the people it was built for lose everything. Please, follow the way of Algiz and protect yourself. Do so by educating yourself. While you still can...

†◊A UNITED WHITE RACE WILL PUT (((THEM))) IN THEIR PLACE◊†

IF THEY ARE STILL AVAILABLE, PLEASE LOOK INTO THE FOLLOWING:

en.wikipedia.org/wiki/Gun_politics_in_the_United_States#Security_against_tyranny
en.wikipedia.org/wiki/False_flag
en.wikipedia.org/wiki/Nepotism
en.wikipedia.org/wiki/Supremacism#Jewish
http://en.rightpedia.info/w/Loxism
en.wikipedia.org/wiki/Immigration_and_Nationality_Act_of_1965
en.wikipedia.org/wiki/White_Genocide
en.wikipedia.org/wiki/Silent_Holocaust
en.wikipedia.org/wiki/National_Origins_Formula
en.wikipedia.org/wiki/Nazism#Reactionary_or_revolutionary?
en.wikipedia.org/wiki/Zionism
en.wikipedia.org/wiki/Edmond_James_de_Rothschild
en.wikipedia.org/wiki/Edict_of_Expulsion
en.wikipedia.org/wiki/Expulsions_and_exoduses_of_Jews
en.wikipedia.org/wiki/Persecution_of_Jews#Western_and_Christian_antisemitism
en.wikipedia.org/wiki/Anti-Defamation_League
en.wikipedia.org/wiki/NAACP
en.wikipedia.org/wiki/American_Israel_Public_Affairs_Committee

en.wikipedia.org/wiki/Gulag
en.wikipedia.org/wiki/Holodomor
en.wikipedia.org/wiki/Marxism–Leninism
en.wikipedia.org/wiki/Revisionism_(Marxism)
en.wikipedia.org/wiki/Talmud
en.wikipedia.org/wiki/Moloch
en.wikipedia.org/wiki/Portal:Judaism
en.wikipedia.org/wiki/Antisemitism#Causes
en.wikipedia.org/wiki/Freemasonry
en.wikipedia.org/wiki/Crusades
en.wikipedia.org/wiki/Barbary_slave_trade

en.wikipedia.org/wiki/Central_bank
en.wikipedia.org/wiki/First_Bank_of_the_United_States
en.wikipedia.org/wiki/Second_Bank_of_the_United_States
en.wikipedia.org/wiki/Federal_Reserve
en.wikipedia.org/wiki/Federal_Reserve_Act
en.wikipedia.org/wiki/Usury
en.wikipedia.org/wiki/Loan_shark
en.wikipedia.org/wiki/Gold_standard

en.wikipedia.org/wiki/Chronology_of_the_universe
en.wikipedia.org/wiki/Timeline_of_the_far_future
en.wikipedia.org/wiki/Ultimate_fate_of_the_universe#Theories_about_the_end_of_the_universe
en.wikipedia.org/wiki/Sun
en.wikipedia.org/wiki/Greenhouse_and_icehouse_Earth
en.wikipedia.org/wiki/Stefan–Boltzmann_law
en.wikipedia.org/wiki/Thermal_radiation

en.wikipedia.org/wiki/Carbon_dioxide_in_Earth's_atmosphere
en.wikipedia.org/wiki/Kardashev_scale
en.wikipedia.org/wiki/Energy_harvesting#Blood_sugar
en.wikipedia.org/wiki/Dyson_sphere
en.wikipedia.org/wiki/Quantum_fluctuation
en.wikipedia.org/wiki/Formation_and_evolution_of_the_Solar_System
en.wikipedia.org/wiki/Biomagnetism

en.wikipedia.org/wiki/Aristotle
en.wikipedia.org/wiki/Plato
en.wikipedia.org/wiki/Socrates
en.wikipedia.org/wiki/Nikola_Tesla
en.wikipedia.org/wiki/Walter_Russell
en.wikipedia.org/wiki/Viktor_Schauberger

en.wikipedia.org/wiki/Mercury_(element)#Medicine
en.wikipedia.org/wiki/Fluoride#Applications
en.wikipedia.org/wiki/Weather_modification
en.wikipedia.org/wiki/Human_overpopulation
en.wikipedia.org/wiki/Pharmaceutical_industry#Pharmaceutical_fraud
en.wikipedia.org/wiki/Herbicide#Health_and_environmental_effects
en.wikipedia.org/wiki/Glyphosate#Toxicity

en.wikipedia.org/wiki/Human#Transition_to_modernity
en.wikipedia.org/wiki/Human_genetic_variation#Population_genetics
en.wikipedia.org/wiki/Human_taxonomy#Subspecies
en.wikipedia.org/wiki/Race_and_genetics#Race_and_medicine
en.wikipedia.org/wiki/Portal:Cannabis
en.wikipedia.org/wiki/Proprioception
en.wikipedia.org/wiki/List_of_primates_by_population
en.wikipedia.org/wiki/List_of_carnivorans_by_population
en.wikipedia.org/wiki/Human_population_planning
en.wikipedia.org/wiki/Dred_Scott_v._Sandford
en.wikipedia.org/wiki/Treason#United_States
en.wikipedia.org/wiki/Attainder#Corruption_of_blood

Correct Your Status:
tasa.americanstatenationals.org

Woodrow Wilson's "The New Freedom":
gutenberg.org/files/14811/14811-h/14811-h.htm

Henry Ford's "The International Jew":
gutenberg.org/cache/epub/37539/pg37539-images.html

"The Greatest Story Never Told":
thegreateststorynevertold.tv/

For more information about the Elder Futhark and Runes, please visit:
runesecrets.com

PERICULUM IN MORA.